Kathleen's Enduring Faith

BOOK FOUR
of the
A Life of Faith:
Kathleen McKenzie
Series

TRACY LEININGER CRAVEN

MCP
Mission City Press
Franklin, Tennessee

Book Four of the *A Life of Faith: Kathleen McKenzie* Series

Kathleen's Enduring Faith
Copyright © 2007, Tracy Leininger Craven. All Rights Reserved.

Published by Mission City Press, Inc.

Cover & Interior Design: Richmond & Williams
Typesetting: BookSetters

Unless otherwise indicated, all Scripture references are from the Holy Bible, New International Version (NIV). Copyright © 1973, 1978, 1984 by International Bible Society. Used by permission of Zondervan Publishing House, Grand Rapids, MI. All rights reserved.

Kathleen McKenzie and *A Life of Faith* are trademarks of Mission City Press, Inc.

For more information, write to Mission City Press at 202 Second Avenue South, Franklin, Tennessee 37064, or visit our Web Site at: **www.alifeoffaith.com.**

For a FREE catalog call 1-800-840-2641.

Library of Congress Catalog Card Number: 2006930440
Craven, Tracy Leininger
    Kathleen's Enduring Faith
    Book Four of the *A Life of Faith: Kathleen McKenzie* Series
    ISBN-13: 978-1-928749-28-8
    ISBN-10: 1-928749-28-3

Printed in the United States of America
2 3 4 5 6 7 8 — 11 10 09 08

DEDICATION

To my husband, David, for his unfailing love and support and to our precious daughter Elaina Hope.

PRESIDENT HOOVER'S DROUGHT RELIEF PROGRAM

*A*s corporate America struggled to survive the stock market crash, the farmers in the Midwest were experiencing a problem of their own—drought. Between April of 1930 and March of 1931, the state of Ohio had only 21.93 inches of rain, making it one of the driest twelve-month periods in Ohio's history. President Hoover organized drought relief for the struggling farmers through the Federal Farm Board, the American Red Cross, and the National Drought Relief Committee. Despite this organized relief, many farmers lost their crops and all they owned—including their farms.

SEASONAL MEAL MENU LIVING OFF THE LAND

Because the McKenzie family lived off the land, their meals consisted mostly of food they grew in their gardens or gathered from their livestock. Staples like sugar, flour, and baking soda were bought or bartered for at their local dry goods or general store in Archbold, Ohio. The extra eggs from their laying hens and the surplus cream from the Jersey cows were "as good as gold" when it came to trading.

Winter meals consisted of soups and stews made with home-canned vegetables from their garden and some kind of meat—venison, which they had hunted, or pork, chicken, or, on rare occasions, beef, which they had raised for butchering. By the end of winter, the fruits and vegetables that had been canned during the previous summer and fall were almost gone.

Spring brought with it the hope of new life. Soon, tender fresh vegetables grew in the garden and the McKenzies had onions to flavor their meals. There was also fresh rhubarb for pies and pastries.

In summer their table was filled with fresh vegetables from the garden. What they didn't eat was canned for the next winter.

During the fall harvest, the remainder of fruits and vegetables were gathered and dried, canned, and stored away. Bushels of apples and potatoes were put "down cellar" where they stayed fresh for several months. Livestock was butchered and hung in the smokehouse. The fields were harvested; the barns were filled with hay and grains for the livestock. The final preparations for winter were made with the hope that the harvest would see them through to next spring.

Ku Klux Klan

Following the Civil War, the Republicans in Congress established the Freeman's Bureau and the Reconstruction Act to give former slaves voting

rights, educational opportunities, and health care. The Ku Klux Klan was started in May of 1866, in Pulaski, Tennessee, by a group of men who were outraged at these rights. Many of the leaders of the KKK were former members of the Confederate army. The KKK ravaged many of the Southern states—harassing people, destroying property, and even killing people. They targeted black men and women, whites who were sympathetic toward the blacks, and anyone whom the KKK felt was responsible for supporting the Republicans in Congress that passed these laws. By the 1920s, the Klan targeted blacks, Catholics, Jews, Socialists, and anyone they viewed as a foreigner. The KKK existed as far north as Ohio and as far west as Oregon.

McKenzie Family Tree

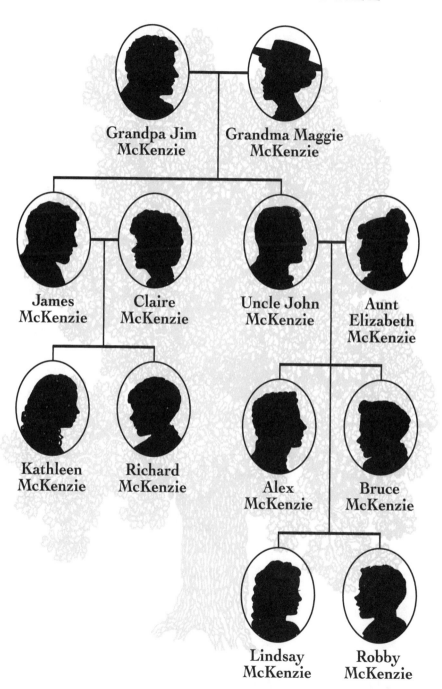

SETTING

The winter of 1930 has melted into one of the most devastating droughts in Ohio's history, and the McKenzie family now struggles to keep the summer crops alive at Stonehaven, the family farm in Archbold, Ohio.

CHARACTERS

 THE MCKENZIE HOUSEHOLD ∞

James McKenzie — Age 35, Kathleen's father
Claire McKenzie — Age 32, Kathleen's mother
Their children:
    Kathleen McKenzie — Age 12
    Richard McKenzie — Age 9

Grandma Maggie and Grandpa Jim McKenzie — Kathleen's grandparents

Aunt Elizabeth and Uncle John McKenzie — Kathleen's aunt and uncle, and their children:
    Alex — Age 18, Kathleen's cousin
    Bruce — Age 15, Kathleen's cousin
    Lindsay — Age 14, Kathleen's cousin
    Robby — Age 8, turning 9, Kathleen's cousin

∞ OTHERS ∞

Lucy Meier — Age 12, Kathleen's best friend in Fort Wayne, Indiana
Peter Meier — Age 14, Lucy's brother

Dr. and Mrs. Schmitt — Family doctor and his wife, friends of the McKenzies and parents of:

> **Freddie Schmitt** — Schoolmate and friend of Kathleen

Mr. and Mrs. Johnston — Neighbors and owner of the dog Old Bruiser, and suspected members of the Ku Klux Klan

Mr. and Mrs. Williams — The McKenzie family's new neighbors who just moved to the Ohio farm country from the South, and parents of:

> **Sharly** — Age 13
> **Emma** — Age 10
> **Elias** — Age 8
> **Tara Lee** — Age 6
> **Sammy** — Age 3
> **Earl** — Age 8 months

Pastor and Mrs. Scott — The McKenzie family's Ohio pastor and his wife, and their son:

> **William** — Age 16

Sheriff Ratcliff — Archbold, Ohio, town sheriff

Dr. Rogers — Family doctor of Kathleen's relatives and grandfather to:

> **Victoria** — Age 6

A Surprise Visitor

Delight yourself in the LORD and he will give you the desires of your heart. Commit your way to the LORD; trust in him and he will do this: He will make your righteousness shine like the dawn, the justice of your cause like the noonday sun.

PSALM 37:4–6

Kathleen sat down the water bucket she was hauling to brush her sweaty hair out of her face. With her hand she shielded the scorching late afternoon sun from her eyes and searched the horizon for any sign of rain. But there was nothing to give her hope. Not even the faintest wisp of a cloud. Kathleen picked the bucket back up and headed to the barn to put one last bucket of water in the horses' trough. Summer at Stonehaven had proved to be much hotter than Kathleen could have ever imagined possible. She was glad that her barn chores were almost completed for the day. Now all Kathleen had to do was milk the two Jersey cows, Clover and Anna Belle.

One month had passed since Robby and she had become lost while looking for the cows. As Kathleen milked the cows, her thoughts drifted to the frightful events of that evening. The unsettling images of the Ku Klux Klan ceremony they had stumbled upon still burned vividly in her memory. Papa and Kathleen had gone to town the very next morning to report to Sheriff Ratcliff what she had witnessed and how they believed that Mr. Johnston was involved.

"I've had my suspicions of such activity recently, but until now, I haven't had anything to confirm it," the sheriff had said. "I'll look into it immediately and keep my eyes open for any more mischief. I just hope we can settle things before something bad happens. It's unfortunate that any of the folks around here are involved or even associated with such a movement." He shook his head. "There's no telling what harm they could do."

Afterward, the McKenzie family made a special effort to make the Williams family feel welcome in their community. But earning the Williamses' trust and friendship turned out to be difficult. Though they were kind and gratefully accepted the McKenzies' visits to drop off some of Grandma Maggie's famous sugar cookies or a fresh buttermilk pie, and though they appeared to enjoy their evenings at Stonehaven for dinner or an evening quilting bee, it took time for their guarded behavior to melt away. Slowly, as the heat of summer evaporated the last bit of moisture in the air, the Williamses became open and at ease with the McKenzies. It turned out to be a good thing for both families. Not only did they find new friendships, but they were able to help each other through the drought, one of the worst that Grandpa McKenzie could ever remember. Both farms were suffering, and they were able to share skills, farming insights, and resources. Even so, it was turning into a long, hot summer.

Kathleen stopped milking Anna Belle for a moment and gently patted her side.

"Even you can tell it's hot, can't you? You're producing half the milk you did a month ago." The gentle, brown-eyed Jersey cow looked back at her and mooed as if to defend herself. "I know! I know! It's not your fault." Kathleen laughed and began milking again. She had almost finished when Kathleen heard footsteps rush up behind her. Before she could turn around, someone's hands were over her eyes.

"Guess who?"

Kathleen immediately recognized her papa's voice, but the hands were too dainty and soft to be his. Kathleen sat for a brief moment and then she heard a familiar laugh. It sounded like Lindsay, but it could

not be because she was in the chicken coop gathering eggs. Kathleen could hear the hens squawk and cluck angrily as Lindsay removed the eggs from their nests.

It quickly dawned on Kathleen who this was.

"Lucy?" Kathleen turned and found herself looking into the face of her dearest friend. She put aside her milk bucket and gave Lucy a big hug.

"I can't believe you're really here! I had completely given up hope of seeing you!" Kathleen exclaimed. "Why didn't you tell me you were coming in one of your letters?"

"I wanted to surprise you!" Lucy's smile was the same and her eyes were as sparkling blue as ever and she still wore her blonde curls shoulder length, but she had lost weight and looked frail.

"I almost didn't recognize you with your new hairdo," said Lucy.

"Yes, I know I look different." Kathleen's face grew hot. Her hand went to her short hair. It had been a couple of months now since the hair-curling incident, but it was still shorter than Lucy had ever seen it. Kathleen had almost forgotten about her shorter hair.

"You wrote and told me about it, but I had no idea how cute it would look. All the girls are getting their hair cut like that in the city. Even my sisters."

"Really?" Kathleen knew how stylish Lucy's sisters were and up to that point she thought Lucy was just trying to make her feel better.

"Really."

Kathleen heard the door to the chicken coop creak open and then shut. She grasped Lucy's hand. "Come, you must meet my cousin Lindsay. Then she and I can show you all around Stonehaven." She pulled Lucy toward the other end of the barn where Lindsay was about to shovel out her horses' stall.

Kathleen stopped. "Oh, I forgot all about poor Anna Belle." She looked pleadingly at her father.

He grabbed the milk pail. "You girls go on. I'll finish milking her," Papa said as he squatted on the milk stool.

"Thank you, Papa." Kathleen ran back and hugged his neck. "You're the best father in the whole world."

Papa pressed his head against Anna Belle's side and began milking her. The stream of milk pinged as it hit the side of the bucket. "By the way, Lucy gets to stay for three weeks—so you'll have plenty of time to show her around." He looked at Lucy. "Remember the doctor's orders. No overexerting yourself."

"Yes, sir, I promise to be good," Lucy said.

"I'll take good care of her," Kathleen said as she led Lucy to Doll and Nellie's stall in search of Lindsay.

Lucy's first two weeks on the farm passed quickly. Lindsay and Lucy became friends instantly, and the three girls spent every spare moment riding horses,

swinging on the giant tire swing in front of the house, or playing with Sunshine and Samson, the two new barn kittens Bruce had brought home from town as a surprise for Lindsay and Kathleen. One night, the girls even camped out in Lindsay's hayloft hideout.

One afternoon, while Lucy, Lindsay, and Kathleen were helping to cook dinner, Aunt Elizabeth suddenly stopped kneading the dough for bread and looked out the window. Her face showed a deep sadness. "Here it is midsummer and I still haven't finished my spring-cleaning!" Aunt Elizabeth wiped the flour on her hands off onto her starched blue and yellow floral feed sack apron. She ran her finger across the windowsill. "Just look at that dust! And those windows! I've never seen them so dirty."

Kathleen cringed at the word *spring-cleaning*. Her mother was so particular and worked her so hard during that time of year that she dreaded even the mention of it. Kathleen glanced over at Lindsay to see if she had heard. Lucy and she were peeling potatoes at the other end of the kitchen and talking about Blue, Bruce's pig that he hoped would win the grand prize at the county fair.

"If Bruce wins the prize money, he plans to put it in his savings so he can go to seminary someday," Lindsay said.

"My brother, Peter, wants to go to college too. He is working hard to save every penny—his dream is to become a doctor." Lucy's eyes brightened as she spoke of her brother. Kathleen brought her attention back to Aunt Elizabeth who was still talking about spring-cleaning.

"Where has the time gone? Whatever am I going to do?" Aunt Elizabeth sounded discouraged. Normally she was energetic, and joy seemed to spring from a never-ending well inside her heart.

Kathleen added more flour to the gooey dough she'd been kneading and worked it in with her hands. It troubled her to see Aunt Elizabeth even a little bit sad or tired; she had been so good to her and to her family.

Kathleen thought back to when they first moved to Stonehaven Farm. Papa had told her that the crop prices had not been as good the last few years. This year they had planted more than ever before with high hopes for the fall harvest. Now it was nearing the end of June and they had not felt a drop of rain for several weeks. Grandpa had said that the cornfields should be "knee high by the fourth of July." Judging by the withered little shoots that poked up here and there, that would be impossible.

Kathleen had never thought about the importance of rain before; she assumed that they would plant the fields and gardens and it would come pouring down. Now that she and Lindsay had to haul buckets of water from the pump to the vegetable garden every morning,

Kathleen understood. She decided she had better start praying for rain, not only during her morning devotions, but also all throughout the day. Lucy helped them spread straw around the plants and between the rows to hold in the moisture. She wanted to haul water too, stating that she felt stronger now than she had in months. Even though she did look better and had even gained some weight, Kathleen would not hear of it. Lucy was supposed to be taking it easy.

Before long it dawned on Kathleen that if it did not rain soon, they might lose the entire wheat and corn crops. She had tried to help out wherever she could, trying to ease the burden. But each day without rain made the day's work seem harder for the whole family. Lucy's cheerful personality and evident growing health did brighten their days, but an ominous cloud hung over the entire family that could only be dissolved by rain.

The general feeling of discouragement was never voiced, and for the most part, life continued as usual. It was just an occasional sigh or strained tone of voice that hinted at the burden the adults carried. Kathleen wanted to make everything turn out right for her relatives and for her papa. Since the crops had been planted, he had spent countless unsuccessful weeks back in Fort Wayne looking for work. Kathleen missed him when he was gone, but she knew there wasn't money to travel back and forth often.

Kathleen sighed. Now Aunt Elizabeth was discouraged, and she wanted so much to find a way to encourage her.

"I need to go to town tomorrow morning to do some shopping," Aunt Elizabeth said, interrupting Kathleen's thoughts. "Your mother says she wants to use the telephone at Jensen's General Store to call your papa in Fort Wayne."

Kathleen's heart jumped. She hoped that Aunt Elizabeth was about to invite her to join them. It would be wonderful to hear Papa's voice. He always made her feel better. He had been gone nearly three weeks—the longest they had ever been apart. Maybe he would have news of a job by now.

Kathleen wondered if she dared hope. Lucy had brought stories of home and had stirred up her desire to be back in Fort Wayne. When the summer turned hot like this, Papa would take her to Mrs. Sweet's Ice Cream and Soda Shoppe downtown. He would buy her a cold root beer float or strawberry malt. She also thought about last summer when Lucy and she had played for hours in the tree house down by the river where it was cool.

Kathleen finished kneading the dough and shaped it into loaves. She was enjoying Lucy's visit so much. She could not imagine having to say good-bye again.

In the past year Kathleen had lived two different lives in two different centuries—from a city life of ease to a primitive country life of hard work, sweat, and no running water or electricity. The amazing thing about living on the farm was that though they worked twice as hard, they were poorer than ever before. Even so, Kathleen loved Stonehaven.

Everyone played an important part in operating the farm. It took each person pitching in to accomplish the day's work. They had all worked together to get the crops and gardens planted. Each day the men worked the fields; the women cooked, cleaned, and worked in the vegetable garden; and the children cared for the animals. Never before had Kathleen felt so close to her family or had the comforting feeling that no matter what trials lay ahead, not only her parents but now her extended family would be there to love and support her. But most of all, Kathleen knew that God was there to provide for their every need. She had found that life did not always turn out exactly the way she thought it would, but Kathleen was learning to trust God, even when things didn't make sense.

Aunt Elizabeth took the dough, placed it in a greased pan, covered it with a dishcloth, and set it in a warm spot where it would rise. Then she gathered the mixing bowl and measuring cups and brought them to the kitchen sink to wash.

"I was thinking about bringing Grandma to town with us. Other than for church on Sunday, she seldom

gets out these days." She stopped washing dishes and looked out the window where Grandma Maggie and Mama were weeding the garden. Grandma Maggie, wearing her large brimmed straw gardening hat, was watering each plant by hand from a small pail. She stopped, reached out, and touched a dried-up bud. It fell to the ground. She shook her head sadly.

Aunt Elizabeth glanced up at the sky as if searching for rain and then went back to washing the dishes. "I hate to leave the menfolk to fend for themselves," Aunt Elizabeth said, more to herself than to anyone else.

Kathleen's mind raced. She had the perfect idea . . . if only she could convince Mama and Aunt Elizabeth.

"We could do it," Kathleen burst out. "Lindsay, Lucy, and I. We could get supper on. What do you think, girls?" Kathleen looked over at Lindsay and Lucy who were just finishing peeling potatoes.

"We could do what?" Lindsay asked, looking doubtful.

Kathleen explained her idea. As she did, Lindsay shook her head.

Lucy, however, nodded hers. "I think it's a wonderful idea. I've been cooking with my mama recently—she says I'm becoming quite proficient."

"I don't know. It's a lot of work." Lindsay put the potato peelings in a container to be taken out to the pigs.

Kathleen's Enduring Faith

"Come on, Lindsay, we can do it," said Kathleen.

"We've never cooked a whole meal all by ourselves," Lindsay replied.

Kathleen was surprised at how hesitant Lindsay was. "We've done almost everything and with Lucy's help . . ." Kathleen's voice trailed off.

Aunt Elizabeth stopped washing the dishes and stared at Kathleen. After a moment's thought, she shrugged. "I don't see why you girls couldn't handle being in charge of the house and kitchen for one afternoon. Kathleen, I think that's a wonderful idea."

Kathleen's Ambitious Idea

Finally, brothers, whatever is true, whatever is noble, whatever is right, whatever is pure, whatever is lovely, whatever is admirable—if anything is excellent or praiseworthy—think about such things.
PHILIPPIANS 4:8

Early the next morning, the wagon carrying Mama, Aunt Elizabeth, and Grandma Maggie slowly bumped down the dirt drive toward town. All the children were lined up on the porch watching them go.

As soon as the wagon was out of the driveway, Robby and Richard disappeared in the direction of the barn.

"I can't believe we were able to convince my mom that we could handle the house and dinner all by ourselves," said Lindsay as she waved to her mother one last time before the wagon disappeared in the dust

25

cloud kicked up by the horses. "She's never left me here alone without Grandma Maggie to help."

"We had no choice but to convince her." Kathleen grabbed Lindsay's and Lucy's hands.

Lucy raised an eyebrow. "What do you mean, Kathleen? I don't like that look in those green eyes. Why didn't we have a choice?"

"Oh dear! I've seen that look before," Lindsay said. "What's going on in that head of yours?"

"Nothing mischievous and I promise that it will not be hazardous to our appearance." Kathleen let go of their hands. She knew that Lindsay was thinking of the time she curled her hair. "I do have a plan though. It's a surprise for Aunt Elizabeth, Grandma Maggie, and my mama, and I knew that it would never work if they were here."

"A surprise?" Lindsay raised her eyebrow and glanced sideways at Kathleen as they turned to go back inside the kitchen door. "Kathleen McKenzie, what do you have up your sleeve this time? It better not have anything to do with hair-curling formulas." Lindsay ran her fingers through her short hair.

"My goodness—that was harsh," Lucy said. "I told you that short hair is stylish in the city. They call it a 'bob'."

"My idea isn't anything like that." Kathleen picked up the broom from the kitchen pantry and swept it across the floor with a dramatic flair as if she

were dancing with it. "Even though my last mistake did end up being stylish, this surprise doesn't have anything to do with vanity—I've learned my lesson once and for all!"

"Okay, in that case I'll listen," Lindsay said, trying to keep a straight face. Even though her Easter Sunday had been thoroughly humiliating, Kathleen could tell that Lindsay was finally able to see the humor in the mishap.

"Do tell us, Kathleen. Are we going to plan a barn dance and have broomsticks as partners?" Lucy took the broom from Kathleen and curtsied as if she were introducing herself to her new dancing companion.

Kathleen laughed at Lucy's joke. "No, it's much more serious than one of my creative make-believe ideas. I've been thinking a lot about how hard Aunt Elizabeth has been on herself because she hasn't had time to do spring-cleaning. The fact that there has not been any rain makes things worse. I see worry in your mother's eyes each time she brushes the dust off the windowsill or wipes off the shelves." Kathleen paused and looked Lindsay straight in the eye. "Your parents are worried about the crops, aren't they?" Kathleen's voice was sober now. She knew that it was an uncomfortable subject for Lindsay to talk about. For some reason none of them seemed to feel the freedom to talk about hard times. It was almost as if they were afraid it would come across as complaining. They just worked each day with a positive attitude.

"How did you know?" Lindsay's eyes were full of concern.

"I see it in the way your father scans the horizon each morning, hoping to see any sign of rain, and in the way he shakes his head and wipes the sweat off his face at the end of the day." Kathleen's voice drifted off as she looked out the kitchen window. She had been diligent to pray for rain, but it seemed as if God wasn't hearing her prayers. Kathleen scolded herself for even thinking that. She straightened her shoulders with determination.

Lindsay sighed. "I'm afraid you're right. Even though they never talk about it, they are concerned."

"I'm sorry, Lindsay. I didn't mean to bring up a sore subject. It's just that I have a grand idea to help boost our mothers' spirits a bit . . . and Grandma's too." Kathleen ran to the pantry and was back in a moment carrying several buckets, dust rags, the rug beater, and the mop. Lindsay and Lucy looked at her with disbelief as she put the cleaning supplies down. "It will take a lot of work—you and Lucy will have to be totally on board with the idea. We'll even have to get Robby and Richard to pitch in and help."

A smile broke out on Lucy's face as she began to understand Kathleen's train of thought.

Lindsay put her hands on her hips. "Kathleen McKenzie, I don't know what you are up to but some-how—I don't understand how—you've convinced me even before I know what I'm getting myself into. So, whatever it is that you're proposing, if you think it will lift my mom's spirits, I'm up for it."

"Good! I'm glad you feel that way, because attempting to spring-clean two houses in one day is going to be a gigantic task." Kathleen handed Lindsay the rug beater. The look of surprise on Lindsay's face made Kathleen laugh. She could tell it was the last thing Lindsay had expected.

"What! That's crazy," Lindsay said, holding the rug beater like it was a snake. "Spring-cleaning? That will take forever. It's a nice thought, but that's all."

"I think it's a grand idea," said Lucy. She grabbed one of the buckets and swung the mop up on her shoulder. "We can do it! I'd be happy to help, and I can clean just as fast as anyone. Where do I start?"

"No, no way. It's impossible!" Lindsay marched to the pantry and put the rug beater back on its hook.

"Maybe it is, but it's too late to back out now." Kathleen followed her to the pantry and took the rug beater back off the hook. "You already said you'd be up to it if I thought it would bless our moms. Lindsay, just think how much it would mean to them to come home and find both houses dust free and sparkling from the kitchen floor to the upstairs windows." She handed the beater back to Lindsay. "I know it will be a lot of hard work—we can do it. Imagine their happy expressions when they return!" Kathleen clapped her hands together and skipped around the kitchen.

Lindsay looked at the rug beater and then up at Kathleen, slowly shaking her head back and forth. "You *are* crazy—but I guess it won't hurt to try."

The girls quickly wrote down a list of their daily chores plus the individual tasks that spring-cleaning entailed. Then they divided them up evenly. Kathleen read the complete list out loud and shook her head with a determined smile.

"I can clean Grandma's house, if you and Lucy can take care of this house and get the meals on. Richard and Robby will have to water and weed the gardens and do a few extra chores."

"What about feeding the chickens and the cows, and Nellie and Doll need their stall cleaned out?" asked Lindsay. "That's a lot of work for the boys."

Kathleen looked out the window toward the barnyard where the boys were slopping the sow and her large litter of ten piglets. The hungry sow eyed the slop bucket with extra eagerness as Richard and Robby carefully hoisted the bucket over the fence and poured it into the wooden trough below.

"You're right, it is a lot to ask, but I think Robby and Richard can handle the extra work just this once," Kathleen said, with growing enthusiasm. "All they

really need to do is finish feeding a few of the barn animals, let the horses out to pasture, clean all the stalls, and do the garden work. Alex and Bruce already fed most of the animals and milked the cows early this morning before they headed out to work in the fields.

"And I can handle the rest." Kathleen wrote a couple of more things on the growing list of chores. "I'll start at Grandma's. I'll have the boys help me move the mattresses outside to air, and then I'll wash all the linens and hang them out to dry. After that I'll beat the rugs and scrub the floors until they gleam — or maybe I should dust the house and then do the floors." Kathleen took a deep breath. "I should be done by noon. I'll meet you back here in the kitchen so I can help you and Lucy put lunch on for the men."

"Then after lunch, all we'll have to do is wash all the windows, bring the rugs and mattresses back in the house, make up the beds, and start dinner." Lucy studied the list on the table. "Are you sure we're going to get all of this done by five o'clock?"

Kathleen grabbed the list. "I'm sure. But we have to get started now. Won't our mothers be delighted when they come home to a clean house and a warm meal?"

The morning flew by as the girls busily cleaned, each immersing herself in her designated tasks. Kathleen was dusting Grandma Maggie's parlor furniture and windowsills when she spotted the gramophone Grandpa

had given his bride for their twenty-fifth wedding anniversary.

"Music! That's exactly what I need to make this job enjoyable," Kathleen said. "I've missed listening to the radio so much!" She quickly wound the gramophone and twirled about the room to a lively waltz. Soon the parlor was finished, and she moved on to dusting the rest of the house with a skip in her step and a heart as light as a feather.

With Richard's help, Kathleen moved the mattresses into the yard and put the water on to boil for the wash. She had accomplished all this before Lindsay and Lucy had finished removing the mattresses from the big house. Of course, Grandma's house only had two double beds and Uncle John's had twice as many, plus two beds in the boys' room.

Kathleen looked out Grandma's kitchen window and watched Lindsay and the boys slowly carrying Uncle John and Aunt Elizabeth's large mattress out the back door. She quickly turned to the large cast-iron stove and pushed the pot of hot water off the front burner to the back of the stove where it was cooler, then rushed out the back door to help.

Lindsay sighed with relief when they finally got the mattress out the door, across the yard, and propped against the fence. Kathleen smiled with satisfaction.

"Lucy is almost done dusting," Lindsay said.

"Wonderful!" said Kathleen. "The wash water is almost ready. Why don't you beat the last two mattresses while I set up the washtubs and scrub board on Grandma's back porch? If we work together, I'm sure we'll have it done in no time. And we'll use less lye soap. You know how Grandma is with her homemade soap. If we use more than a thin shaving, she'll notice."

Lindsay nodded her head knowingly. "Yes, Grandma cuts such a tiny sliver off the soap bar it's almost impossible to scrub the wash hard enough to actually get suds. Sometimes I think our clothes would last longer if we didn't scrub them so hard. I've always been too scared to use more for fear Grandma would notice and dock my bath soap allowance to make up for what she felt I'd wasted in the wash," Lindsay said with a playful smile.

Kathleen burst into laughter. Lindsay hardly ever cracked even the slightest joke.

"That would be bad," Kathleen said. "Can you imagine going to church on Sunday without a proper Saturday night bath? What would the pastor's son think?"

Lucy walked out of the house. "Is that the handsome young man I saw you talking to last Sunday at church? William, I think his name was." She handed Kathleen a pile of linens. "I've finished dusting."

"That's enough, both of you! Besides, I wasn't talking to him—he merely said good-day—and I nodded in

reply. Now, no more talk about William. We need to get back to work." Lindsay tried to sound serious as she went back inside the house, but for some reason her cheeks were red and she was smiling broadly.

Kathleen knew better. Kathleen had watched William and Lindsay whenever they were together. Lindsay's inability to look at him and her sudden rush of color and William's obvious interest in her cousin had convinced her that their feelings were mutual, even though William was three years older.

It was too bad they were both so young, Kathleen thought to herself. They would make such a cute couple if only they were old enough to court. But what was she doing daydreaming about love stories, when she had so much work to do. Maybe Mama was right when she had told her she was a romantic—although, Kathleen was only a romantic when it came to matching up other people. As for herself, she could not imagine falling in love. That is, not until she was much, much older.

3

Spring-Cleaning

Be joyful in hope, patient in affliction, faithful in prayer.
ROMANS 12:12

Kathleen carefully carried the kettle of hot water to Grandma Maggie's porch and poured the water into the washtub. She turned her head to keep the hot steam off her face. Before long Lindsay and Lucy came out of the house with their arms full of bed linens.

The wash took a little longer than the girls thought, but by noon the clotheslines were graced with a myriad of white linens and colorful quilts and the girls were dragging the large braided rugs outside and were then hanging them over the barnyard fence to give them a sound beating.

"I've beaten lots of rugs, but I have never seen any so dusty." Lucy whacked the braided rug that normally graced the living room floor with the long flat

35

rug beater. A cloud of dust exploded from the cotton fibers.

"Me either. We sure could use a good rain." Lindsay sneezed.

Kathleen waved away the dust with her hand and turned her face the other direction. Out in the field, she saw several men walking toward them, one guiding a horse. "Gracious sakes!" Kathleen exclaimed as she dropped the rug beater and put her hand over her mouth in surprise. "It's noon! The men are coming in from the field. We haven't set out their lunch!"

"Oh, no! Where has the time gone?" Lindsay threw the rug beater on the ground and sprinted toward the kitchen.

"I can help the two of you set out lunch," Lucy offered, rubbing dust from her eyes. Kathleen noticed Lucy looked a bit fatigued, and it occurred to her that the dust and deep cleaning were not good for her lungs.

"That's a great idea, Lucy. I'm not so sure you need to be working so hard in this dust and heat anyway," Kathleen said as they hurried after Lindsay.

The girls dashed about the kitchen attempting to get lunch out before the men arrived from the field. Kathleen noticed that Lucy seemed to do better inside away from the blistering noonday sun. Lucy's health had improved so much since her visit to the farm, and Kathleen wanted it to stay that way.

Spring-Cleaning

"Lucy, maybe you should take a little break after lunch and then you can cook tonight's supper while Lindsay and I finishing cleaning. Can you fry chicken? And bake a cake?"

"Sure I can, but don't you think a cake will take too long? I've never actually made one, but I've watched my mama and sisters make cakes dozens of times and it took a long time," Lucy said as she procured some bread out of the breadbox.

"Lucy is right, and where do you suppose we'll get all the eggs? And what were you saying about a fried chicken? Where do you suppose we'll get fresh meat?" Lindsay asked as she sliced a savory smoked ham for sandwiches.

"From the henhouse, of course. I gathered a lot of eggs last night and I'm sure your mom wouldn't mind if we used the extra ones in a cake — after all, this is going to be a special occasion," Kathleen said as she pulled a large bowl of potato salad out of the icebox. "And as for the fresh meat, I overheard Bruce say that he needed to put one of the hens away because the other chickens had pecked it so much. I've already asked the boys to butcher the poor hen." Just then, the girls heard a terrible squawking noise coming through the open kitchen window from the direction of the barn.

"I think the poor thing is being prepared for frying as we speak," Lucy said, motioning toward the noise.

"Well, if you say so . . . But I can't remember Bruce ever butchering a laying hen just because the other chickens were pecking on her." Lindsay shook her head in uncertainty.

After the noon meal, the girls gave Richard and Robby their next list of chores, only to find that they still had not completed the first batch she'd given them.

"You boys need to hurry." Kathleen put her hands on her hips. "If we're not done by four o'clock, the surprise is ruined."

"We *are* trying hard, but it's a lot of work, Kathleen." Richard dug at a hole in his pants. "Butchering that hen wasn't easy."

"You should have seen the other chickens running around. There were feathers flying everywhere." Robby waved his hands over his head. "I liked diving for the little hen. She was so fast it took us nearly an hour just to catch her—I even ripped my best work shirt." He showed her the tear in the elbow.

Lindsay's face paled during the boy's explanation, but it wasn't until later when Kathleen and she were mixing together a concoction of lye soap, vinegar, and water to make window-washing liquid that Kathleen found out what was troubling her.

"Kathleen, are you sure this is how your mother makes window-washing soap?" Lindsay asked.

"Pretty sure . . . is that what's bothering you? You've looked anxious about something ever since

lunch." Kathleen searched her cousin's face. She could tell by the way she'd been avoiding looking at her that something wasn't right.

"Being from the city and all, I guess you wouldn't know . . ."

"Wouldn't know what, Lindsay? I've been living here for months now and I think I know just about—"

"It's that hen. I'm not so sure that Bruce meant for us to kill her."

Kathleen felt sick to her stomach.

"And for another thing, the chickens don't like being chased like that . . . They're likely to just up and stop laying eggs when they've had a fright like that." Tears welled up in Lindsay's eyes.

What had she done? Without eggs they wouldn't be able to bake any of the normal baked goods or prepare breakfasts the way they did every day at Stonehaven. It wasn't like they could just run up to the corner store and buy more either. In fact, they bartered the extra eggs at the local general store; eggs were as good as gold.

Lindsay brushed the tears away. "It's my fault. I should've stopped you. I know you were just trying to do something special. I just don't want to add one more burden to my family."

"No, it's my fault. I misunderstood. Causing stress is the last thing on my mind right now," Kathleen said, quite sobered. After a moment's thought she perked

up again. "Maybe Richard exaggerated. Maybe they didn't scare them as much as he said. He's always making his adventures sound bigger than they really are."

"I sure hope so," Lindsay said as she stirred the window-washing mixture.

Kathleen hoped so too. The family didn't need for the chickens to stop laying their precious eggs. As Kathleen prayed silently she divided the mixture into two buckets.

Dear Lord, I've really messed things up. Please help the laying hens not to be spooked, and please help us finish the spring-cleaning in time. I so want to bless Aunt Elizabeth and Grandma Maggie. Please help me to be an encouragement to my relatives, not a burden. Amen.

"Do you think we'll finish in time?" Lindsay asked, as if she had heard Kathleen's prayer.

"It will be a close call," Kathleen said as she brushed a strand of red hair out of her face. "Why don't I clean the windows in both houses while you wash the floors? Then all we'll have to do is move the mattresses and rugs back and make up the beds."

"Sounds like a plan," Lindsay said. "Are you sure you know about washing windows?"

"Sure, all you do is apply this mixture to the windows with old newspapers and let it dry—right?" Kathleen asked, looking for reassurance. The last thing she wanted to do was make another mistake.

"I really don't know." Lindsay shrugged. "That's not how my mama does it."

Kathleen, feeling a bit unsure of herself, set to work. She wiped down all the downstairs' windows in her aunt and uncle's house. As she worked, she wondered if she had used the right proportions in her window-washing mixture. Something must be wrong because she didn't remember her mother's windows getting smeared and smudged in black. After Kathleen finished the kitchen window, she could barely see out of it. Kathleen wiped one of the panes harder. It only darkened to an inky gray. Maybe something in the mixture was drawing the ink out of the newspaper . . . or maybe the newspaper was too old.

Lucy had been watching her as she breaded the chicken for dinner. "Are the windows supposed to look like that?" She pointed at the window with a chicken leg.

"I don't remember them looking like this." Kathleen stood back and looked at the mess. "Most likely my mama always went back and wiped them down again with fresh water and a dishrag and I've just forgotten that second step."

"That will probably do the trick," Lucy said, her voice sounding weary. Kathleen glanced over at her and felt a pang of guilt. Was her plan working Lucy too hard? She clearly remembered her papa's command that Lucy was not to overexert herself.

"Are you okay?" she asked.

"Yes, it's just hot in here." Lucy wiped her hand across her brow. "I'll get a glass of cool water from the pump in a little while and I'll feel better."

"I think I'll finish applying the solution, before going back over them with the water." Kathleen pressed on upstairs to the bedrooms. Before long the whole house became dark from the blackened windows. Kathleen picked up her bucket and headed downstairs. As she passed back through the kitchen on her way to the other house, Kathleen found Lucy hard at work peeling potatoes. She looked less fatigued.

"How are things going? Have you already finished quartering and breading the chicken?" Kathleen asked. She tried hard to hide the sense of urgency in her voice—Kathleen knew they were running out of time and wanted to make the most of every second.

"Three o'clock and all is well!" Lucy announced. "The chicken is battered and waiting to be fried and the cake is in the oven."

Kathleen nodded her approval as she hurried out the door. It was three o'clock! That meant she only had one hour to finish the windows, bring the mattresses, rugs, and sheets in, and make up all the beds.

Kathleen rushed across the barnyard to Grandma Maggie's, trying not to trip over the bucket she carried.

Spring-Cleaning

She had nearly finished all the windows when she heard Lucy scream. She looked up and saw a pillar of bright red light flashing in Aunt Elizabeth's kitchen window. Kathleen couldn't tell for sure through the smudged black ink smeared on the window, but the light grew quickly and flickered like a large flame of fire. There was more screaming.

Dear Lord, please protect Lucy, and please don't let the house burn down!

Cleaning Disasters

*Consider it pure joy, my brothers, whenever you face trials
of many kinds, because you know that the testing of your
faith develops perseverance.*
JAMES 1:2–3

Kathleen dropped her window-washing tools and dashed across the barnyard to the kitchen. "Lucy! Lucy, are you okay?" Kathleen burst through the smoke-filled doorway to find Lucy and Lindsay beating the last of what was now a small ring of fire that danced and smattered about the kitchen floor. Kathleen looked up at the ceiling. Black soot clung to a large round, scorched area above the stove.

Richard and Robby clambered through the doorway.

"What happened?" asked Richard. "I could hear you girls screaming clear in the barn."

"I think the grease got a little too hot," said Lucy. She had a black smudge on her face where she'd obviously rubbed it with the back of her hand. "When I saw the flame in the frying pan, I grabbed the pan handle with one hand and my glass of drinking water in the other. My plan was to bring it outside and pour the water on the fire, but the flames got too high before I could reach the door."

"So you poured the water on it?" Lindsay asked.

Lucy nodded. "I thought that would take care of it, but—but that only made things worse." Lucy rubbed a red spot on her wrist.

"You've been scorched!" Kathleen exclaimed. "Robby, fetch some butter from the icebox."

"I'm okay, really," Lucy said.

Kathleen could see pink, raw skin on her friend's wrist and knew Lucy was just being brave.

Lucy looked at Lindsay. "I just don't understand why the water made the oil flame up like that. I thought water put out fires."

"My mom says flour is what puts out oil fires," Lindsay said as she gently turned Lucy's arm to examine it. "But how would you have known? Does your wrist hurt badly?"

"We can't take time to bother with it now; it's getting late. When Robby returns, I can put the butter on by myself," Lucy said.

It took some convincing, but time *was* short, so reluctantly Lindsay and Kathleen both went back to work.

"The kitchen floor is the last one that needs scrubbing in this house—at least that worked out for our benefit." Lindsay shrugged. "I'll go over to Grandma's and scrub her floors and do this one last."

Kathleen followed Lindsay across the yard so she could finish the windows. But as soon as she started back to work, she saw one of the milk cows running wildly through the yard with a pair of Grandma's bloomers hanging from its horns.

"Oh no! Please—please tell me I'm just imagining this," Kathleen moaned.

"Imagining what? Have our moms returned early?" Lindsay looked up from scrubbing the parlor floor.

"No, it's much worse! Anna Belle has gotten mixed up in the laundry. The boys must have left the gate to the field open."

"Oh no—Grandma Maggie's flower garden!" Lindsay dropped her scrub brush, jumped to her feet, and dashed out the door.

Kathleen raced after her.

"Watch out for my wash bucket!" Lindsay called over her shoulder. But it was too late. In her hurry, Kathleen's foot landed on the scrub brush, it slipped out from under her, and she went soaring through the

air, hands and face first, right into the bucket of sudsy water. The bucket tipped and dirty water flooded the parlor's wooden floor.

"I am so sorry!" Kathleen cried.

"It's okay. I can clean that up later—but we have to get Anna Belle. If she damages the roses or vegetable garden we'll be in big trouble," Lindsay said.

Kathleen picked herself up and rushed out the back door. The scene that she beheld was far worse than Kathleen feared. It wasn't just Anna Belle in the yard, but all seven of their milk and beef cows. Richard and Robby had already discovered what had happened and were running blindly behind the cows hollering and waving their arms like a couple of angry geese. Their noble efforts to round them up only resulted in startling the herd and making the situation twice as grim.

"Richard, Robby, stand between the garden and the cows," Kathleen called out. "No matter what happens, you must keep them from trampling through the vegetables."

"We'll try, but this sure would work better if I had a dog," Robby shouted as he and Richard quickly made a wide circle around the herd to position themselves in front of the precious vegetables. They waved their arms and shouted. "Go away." "Shoo."

The cows stopped, looked at them suspiciously, and then veered off in the opposite direction.

Kathleen's Enduring Faith

"Kathleen, look out! They're heading toward the clotheslines," called Lindsay. "We have to turn them."

Kathleen slowed her pace so as not to frighten them anymore.

Lindsay talked softly to the cows as she walked toward them. "Easy, Clover; easy, girl. It's okay, Molly. Here, Anna Belle, I'm not going to hurt you." They instantly settled to a walk and Lindsay gently shooed them back toward the gate that they'd come through.

Kathleen urged them slowly forward. Their plan seemed to be working when Lucy burst out of the kitchen, racing toward the bewildered cows, wielding a broom, and yelling wildly. The herd bolted straight toward the clothesline. Unfortunately, it was situated between the corner of the house and the fence which created a bottleneck. In order to get through, the frightened cows were forced to tear right through the clean white sheets and various white undergarments.

Kathleen stopped and covered her eyes with her hands. "All that hard work—I can't watch." But the hope that they might not do any damage was too tempting. Kathleen cracked her fingers open far enough to see the white linens and bloomers exploding from the line. Most of the sheets and undergarments fell to the ground and were trampled in the stampede. A few unfortunate pieces clung helplessly around the necks or horns of the startled animals and were paraded through the yard.

48

Worse, at that very moment, the family wagon pulled up the drive. Tears welled up in Kathleen's eyes as she glanced around the yard.

She looked from blackened windows, to crazed cows who were racing toward Richard, Robby, and the garden, to the wagon that was bringing her mama, Aunt Elizabeth, and Grandma Maggie closer and closer, and then back again at the sad-looking house windows. Through tears that quickly filled her eyes, Kathleen spotted smoke funneling out of the kitchen door that Lucy had left wide open.

"Oh no! What now?" Kathleen stumbled toward the house, then dashed through the kitchen door and straight for the wood-burning stove that was billowing clouds of black smoke. She opened the oven door and thick smoke billowed out. She coughed and gagged as it filled her lungs and burned her eyes. She stepped back to catch her breath.

When the smoke finally cleared enough for Kathleen to remove the charred contents, she found the smoldering remains of Lucy's cake.

Poor Lucy! She wasn't used to the wood-burning stove. Maybe she could hide the remains in the shrubbery by the back porch—there was already enough evidence of catastrophe around here.

Kathleen turned to dispose of what was left of the charred brick-looking cake and found herself face-to-face with Mama. She froze—all except the tears that

she had forced away moments before. Now they gushed up in her eyes and streamed freely down her cheeks.

"Mama." Kathleen sobbed as she looked into her mother's shocked face. "We—we wanted it to be a sur-surprise," Kathleen sobbed. "And it's turned out horrible. I—I couldn't have even dreamed up a nightmare this b-bad."

Mama grabbed a hot pad and, without a word, took the smoldering cake out of Kathleen's hands. She rushed it outdoors where it could smoke without contaminating the house any further with its unpleasant, burned odor. Kathleen sank onto a kitchen chair and let the tears flow without restraint.

Mama came back into the kitchen and placed her arms around Kathleen. "There now, Kathleen. We can mend whatever wrong has taken place . . . but please dear, do help me understand what sort of surprise you tried to plan . . . and what exactly took place here today."

By the time Kathleen had finished telling Mama all about their good intentions to spring-clean both houses, Lindsay, Lucy, and the boys had secured the cows on the proper side of the fence. Now Lindsay was attempting to explain the same thing to her mother and Grandma Maggie. Mama was particularly interested to know what Kathleen had done to the windows to make them black.

Mama shook her head in wonder as Kathleen explained her special cleaning mixture. "It was the solution you used—the ink could not help but bleed out of the newsprint and smear all over the glass. But never mind that, Kathleen McKenzie, you've attempted an enormous feat with noble intentions—you have nothing to be ashamed of as far as objectives go." As Mama spoke, she scanned the kitchen and the yard to assess the damage. "However, next time I suggest you try to tackle something a bit more manageable—no one, not even I, would expect you girls to complete such a giant task in one day."

"I see that now." Kathleen hung her head. "It sounded so much easier than it turned out to be—I thought how wonderful it would be to surprise Aunt Elizabeth, Grandma Maggie, and you, that I didn't evaluate things well. Now, instead of being a blessing, we've made an embarrassing mess of Stonehaven." Kathleen dabbed at her tears with a handkerchief. "I don't want to be around when the men come home from the fields. I'd rather bury myself in the hay than see the expression on Bruce's face when he sees all this." Kathleen twisted the tear-soaked handkerchief she held in her hand. "There is one more thing, Mama. A bigger blunder than what you've seen." Kathleen sighed in agony. "Yesterday, I overheard Bruce say that one of the new laying hens needed to be taken out because the other hens were pecking on her."

"Yes?" Mama asked, one eyebrow arching.

"I thought he meant killed, so I had Richard and Robby butcher it for dinner."

"Oh dear, I can see how you'd be concerned about that . . . but it's a reasonable mistake. You don't need to worry about Bruce—he'll understand. He thinks highly of you, Kathleen, and you know it."

Mama stood. "Maybe there isn't a need for further embarrassment this time," she said as she tied on a kitchen apron and rolled up her sleeves. "If we all work hard, we might be able to have this place in tip-top shape before sundown. Did I fail to mention that we may be having company tonight?"

"Company! Who?" Kathleen asked.

"We ran into Mrs. Williams and her girls today while we were in town. Aunt Elizabeth invited them over for an evening quilting bee."

"Gracious sakes! We better get things cleaned up around here. I can't wait to see Sharly." Kathleen stood up and grabbed a bucket. "I think I'll start with my specialty— the windows."

5

The Surprise

Share with God's people who are in need. Practice hospitality.
ROMANS 12:13

Mrs. Williams and her three daughters did come over that evening. Much to Kathleen's relief, they were able to host them in a clean, tidy house. Grandma Maggie set up the large quilting frame in her living room. Kathleen and Lindsay set chairs strategically around the frame, so everyone had an area that they could quilt.

The girls visited with Sharly and her younger sisters, Emma and Tara Lee, while they hand-quilted the postage stamp quilt Grandma Maggie had "pieced": She had sewn together hundreds of tiny squares of colorful scraps of material.

"What was this pretty blue and white floral print, Grandma Maggie?" Kathleen pointed to one of the squares.

"Ah, lassie, let me think," Grandma Maggie said, stopping her sewing. She stared at the scrap for a moment and then her eyes lit up. "Oh! That was the bonny tablecloth that your grandpa gave me for our fifteenth wedding anniversary. It was one of my favorites. The corners wore out and frayed over the years until it was not fit to grace my table, so I cut it up and made myself an apron. When that became too stained and worn to wear, I cut out the few good sections that were left and added it to my scrap pile."

"And then you pieced it in your quilt," Sharly's younger sister Emma said as she carefully ran the needle in and out of the material creating a tight quilting stitch.

"Where did you get this bright pink material?" Sharly pointed to a small patch near her.

"Lindsay should be able to tell you about that one." Grandma Maggie nodded toward Lindsay who was sitting directly across from her. "Go ahead, lass. I don't want to tell all the stories."

Lindsay looked over at the small postage-stamp-size square and smiled. "That material came from my first school dress. I was excited when Grandma Maggie made it for me, but I was not so sure about the idea of school. When my mama dropped me off— I cried all day. Finally, Alex brought me home during our lunch break."

"Did you cry because you were afraid of the teacher?" Tara Lee asked, her big brown eyes wide in wonder.

"The teacher was nice, but I was pretty shy when I was younger," Lindsay said.

"See, Tara Lee, there are nice teachers." Sharly patted her sister on the top of her neatly braided black hair. Then she looked at Lindsay. "My Uncle Willis, down in Alabama, used to tell us tales about a stern schoolmaster he had when he was a boy. Ever since then my little sister's been frightened of all school teachers."

"That's terrible!" Kathleen sat straight in her chair. "I've loved all my school teachers. They have taught me so many important things and have all been wonderfully kind. Haven't they?" Kathleen looked over at Lucy.

"Yes, they are all very nice. I can't imagine anyone ever feeling afraid of them," Lucy agreed.

Kathleen thought about her teachers back in Fort Wayne. She missed Miss Brooklin and Miss Black especially. She hoped Papa would find a job in time for them to move back before the fall semester. Kathleen was looking forward to entering the spelling bee again. Maybe she would win the state competition again and have the same opportunity to go to Washington, D.C. for nationals. Kathleen sighed. She had been praying that Papa would get a job for so long

now; she was beginning to lose hope. Kathleen looked across the quilting frame at Mama, who had stopped quilting and was looking at Kathleen with a tender yet strong look that told her not to lose hope. It was as if Kathleen's thoughts were written across her face for all to see. Mama must have heard her sigh.

"All of our teachers in Fort Wayne love Kathleen and miss her very much," Lucy said, interrupting Kathleen's thoughts. "But she'll be back soon—I just know it." Kathleen only smiled. She would try not to lose hope. She was determined to trust God's timing, but it was getting harder to wait patiently as weeks went by without Papa finding a job.

Dear Lord, please strengthen my faith. Help me not to be discouraged.

Kathleen focused her attention back on her stitching. The quilting bee continued until late into the evening. Grandma Maggie told story after story about each little patch of scrap material and what its special use was before it was salvaged and pieced into the colorful quilt before them.

Everyone enjoyed themselves except for cousin Robby, who felt that he had been commandeered into helping out with the quilting. His only comfort was that he was working on a section of the quilt that had puppy dogs printed on it. Robby loved dogs and for some time now he had dreamed of owning his own puppy.

The Surprise

"I wish Elias could have come," Robby sighed. Looking over at Mrs. Williams, he asked, "Do you make the boys in your family help the ladies quilt, too?"

"Sometimes—it all depends on if they've been naughty." She smiled as she worked the needle in and out of the quilt, making tiny, evenly spaced stitches.

"In the McKenzie family," Robby said, as he carefully threaded his needle and tied two tiny knots at the end, "if you are under the age of nine and you want to stay up late at night, you have to work." Robby shook his head in dismay and then his face brightened. "Wait a minute. My birthday is in two weeks. Glory be! I'll never have to touch another quilt in all my life!"

By the end of the evening, Robby discovered that he and Elias shared the same birthday. Unbeknownst to Robby, plans were being formed to have a surprise party for both of them on that day. The birthday celebration would take place during the evening at Stonehaven Farm.

On July 27, 1930, at six o'clock in the evening, the Williamses' wagon pulled up the lane. Robby and Richard ran out to greet them as they always did whenever visitors arrived.

"Happy birthday, Robby!" Elias called from his perch on the wagon's buckboard seat. "We brought you a surprise."

"A surprise—for me?" Robby laughed with joy at the thought of what it might be.

Elias disappeared for a moment into the bed of the wagon. Within a flash he was up again holding a small black-and-white furry object with a pink nose. At first Kathleen thought it looked like a skunk.

Robby, who was nearer the wagon and had a much closer view, let out a cry of delight. "A puppy . . . for me? To be my very own?"

Kathleen's heart felt as though it would burst with gratitude. It was a perfectly wonderful gift! Robby had wanted a dog ever since Kathleen had moved to Stonehaven.

"Our sheepdog, Lady, just had a litter of pups." Mr. Williams grinned. "We thought this one might be able to help you round up the cows."

"Yes, sir, I know he will. Thank you! Thank you!" Robby said. Elias handed Robby the little puppy. They both laughed as it wagged its tail and licked Robby all over his face.

"I think he likes you, Robby. Happy birthday!" Mrs. Williams beamed. She handed their eight-month-old child, Earl, to Mr. Williams and stepped down from the wagon.

"Thank you, ma'am," Robby managed to sputter as the puppy bathed his face with licks from its small pink tongue.

The Surprise

"What's his name going to be?" Elias asked eagerly.

"I think I'll name him Spunky."

"Hello, Spunky. It's nice to meet you." Richard reached out and patted the puppy on its head.

Grandpa, Alex, and Bruce walked out of the barn to join the welcoming committee that had gathered around the wagon. "He's a fine pup," Bruce said. "Elias, if I'm not mistaken, Robby isn't the only birthday boy around."

Kathleen immediately felt bad. They had planned a celebration, but as far as she knew the only gift was a big meal and the fluffy yellow cake with chocolate frosting she and Lucy had baked with Grandma Maggie's help. Kathleen wished they had enough money to buy special gifts for the boys. Here the Williamses, who were no better off financially than her family, had given such a nice gift and they had nothing to offer in return—nothing but their friendship.

"Elias," Bruce said, "why don't you and Robby follow me to the barn? That way you can see your birthday gift before dark."

"A gift for me?" Elias's eyes grew wide. "I've never had a birthday gift—not in all my life."

"Well, this birthday's different. Follow me, boys." Bruce strode toward the barn; Robby, Richard, and Elias followed closely behind.

By now the rest of the family had gathered to greet the Williamses.

"Do come inside." Grandma Maggie smiled at Mrs. Williams, who had picked up baby Earl. Grandma Maggie put her arm around Sharly and her younger sister Emma and led them to the house. "It's hotter than a griddle out here in the sun."

"Can I help carry anything?" Papa said to Mr. Williams, who was unloading a large basket of baked goods from the wagon with one hand and holding their precocious, energetic three-year-old son Sammy's hand with the other.

"Thank you, sir." Mr. Williams handed over the basket.

Kathleen was so curious about what Bruce was up to that she followed him and the younger boys to the barn.

Bruce led them to the pen that held his bottle-fed piglet that he had affectionately named Blue Boy.

Was Bruce going to give Elias his hog? He'd been fattening Blue and prepping him for the county fair for months now. Not a week went by without Bruce announcing Blue's growth and how he was sure Blue would win the prize money at the fair.

"Elias, meet Blue." Bruce waved his hand with exaggerated grandeur. "He's not as pretty as that pup, but if you take good care of him, I guarantee he'll be the prize-winning pig at the county fair this fall."

The Surprise

Kathleen's mouth dropped open; she could not believe what she was hearing. Kathleen knew that Bruce had a tender spot in his heart despite his large frame and teasing nature, but she had no idea how kindhearted and generous he really was.

Elias knelt, reached his hand into the pen, and scratched the pig's pink head. Elias broke into a huge smile. "I — I've never had such a prized possession. Is he really mine? Do I get to bring him home?"

"Blue is all yours if you promise to take good care of him," Bruce said.

Kathleen wasn't sure who had a broader smile, Bruce or Elias. Tears of joy sprung into her eyes. Any man in the county would be proud to own that pig — it was valuable livestock. She knew that Bruce wasn't just giving it to Elias, but to the whole Williams family. Times were tough, not just for the Williamses but for all the farmers in the area.

Kathleen would never forget the look of wonder and amazement in the boys' eyes that day as they admired their birthday gifts, but most of all she would not forget the grateful hearts they exhibited. The evening celebration was perfect in every way — Alex and Bruce had planned all sorts of games for the evening. They pounded iron rods in the backyard so they could play horseshoes and set up an obstacle course and burlap bags for relay races. Kathleen and Lucy almost fell over from laughter as they ran with one leg tied together in the three-legged race. Robby, Richard, and Elias teamed up together for the scavenger hunt and surprised everyone when they beat the other teams.

Grandma Maggie, Aunt Elizabeth, and Mama made a delicious feast for dinner complete with Scottish mince and tatties, fresh dinner rolls, summer corn chowder, creamed spinach, rhubarb pie, and for dessert—birthday cake. It looked and smelled so good that the children had a hard time keeping their eyes closed as Grandpa said grace. Kathleen loved to hear her grandpa's prayers. He was a wise, yet humble, sincere man. When he prayed, he wasn't just talking to an Almighty Being, but the Savior of his soul and his nearest Friend.

After dinner, the parents sat on the porch swing and rocking chairs and talked, while the children, including Bruce and Alex, played hide-and-seek outside. As she hid, Kathleen watched the fireflies flicker here and there, lighting up the sky in their mysterious way.

"The fireflies are so beautiful," Kathleen whispered to Lucy, who was hiding with her at the back of the woodpile. "They remind me of last summer when we played in Kirk's Woods behind our home in Fort Wayne."

"Me too," Lucy said. "We had lots of fun, didn't we?"

The Surprise

"We did have lots of adventures in those woods, especially in my tree house — like the time we camped out and were frightened by that lonely old peacock." Kathleen giggled. "I was so sure we were in grave danger." Kathleen grew quiet. "It makes me miss home."

"You'll be home soon." Lucy reached out and squeezed Kathleen's hand. "I just know you will. I've been praying your papa would get a job soon and I feel certain he will."

Richard ran around the corner of Grandpa and Grandma Maggie's house searching for someone to tag.

"We better make a run for it," Kathleen whispered.

The girls darted out from behind the shadows of the woodpile and dashed around the other side of the house toward base, reaching its safety just in time.

Serious Trouble

*Do not be anxious about anything, but in everything, by prayer
and petition, with thanksgiving, present your requests to God.*
PHILIPPIANS 4:6

The birthday party was perfect in every
way, but one. Papa was going back to
Fort Wayne the following morning and
would be taking Lucy home. Although
Kathleen was glad that Lucy was able to stay a
week longer than originally planned, it was still hard
to think of saying good-bye. It would be so much
easier if Kathleen knew when she would see Lucy
again—if she could just know when or if Papa would
get a job.

Life on the farm the next month proved to be so
busy that Kathleen hardly had time to think of how
much she missed Lucy. The sun rose every morning to
further parch Stonehaven's thirsty fields. Each day

they toted water from the pump in an attempt to moisten the cracked dirt in the garden and refresh the wilted plants. The men worked long hours too, trying to save as much of the wheat and corn crops as possible by bringing troughs full of water up from the river.

One evening Kathleen was finishing weeding the garden when Papa, Uncle John, Grandpa, Alex, and Bruce came in from the fields and went to the nearby pump house to wash up for dinner. Kathleen watched Uncle John as he wearily washed the sweat from his brow and slowly dried his face with his handkerchief. "This is the worst drought I've seen in . . . well, I can't remember one this bad."

"It's the worst I've ever seen and I've lived a good many more years." Grandpa splashed a handful of fresh water from the bucket on his face.

"Here it is, middle of August, and the harvest is supposed to be right around the corner. If we don't get rain soon . . ." Uncle John shook his head in dismay and tucked his handkerchief in the back pocket of his overalls.

"Cheer up, Dad." Bruce clasped his strong hand on his dad's shoulder. "Things do look grim, but we haven't lost the back field yet, and the field between us and the river—it looks better than any in the county."

"You bet it does. All we need is a good rain and it will bounce back." Alex rolled up his sleeves to wash his arms. Then he smiled and flexed his muscles for all to

see. "Besides, hauling water isn't all that bad . . . I bet there isn't a man in the county who will beat the McKenzie boys at arm wrestling at the county fair."

Robby was nearby playing with Spunky and overheard their conversation. "That's right, I've been carrying buckets too." He flexed his little arm muscles so hard that his face turned red. Everyone enjoyed a laugh over the boy's optimism, but Kathleen could tell that deep down they all knew that they needed rain and needed it soon.

After the men went inside for supper, Kathleen pulled one last weed, wiped the dust off her hands on her apron, and headed to the washhouse. She pumped a fresh bucket of water from the little red pump and sank her dry hands into the cool water. Kathleen closed her eyes.

Dear Lord, please let it rain soon.

That evening as the McKenzies were finishing supper, they heard hurried footsteps race across the back porch, then a heavy knock on the kitchen door.

"Hello? Is anybody home?" The frightened voice of a child called out.

Uncle John jumped up to answer.

"Who could it be at this time of night?" Aunt Elizabeth untied her soiled apron as she followed Uncle John to the door.

Kathleen thought she recognized the voice, but she wasn't quite sure. All was silent at the dinner table as everyone strained to hear who it might be.

"Sharly? What is the matter, dear? Why, you're shaking like a leaf," Aunt Elizabeth cried.

Kathleen pushed back her chair and raced through the dining room to the kitchen. Sharly was standing out on the porch, with tears streaming down her face and shaking, just as Aunt Elizabeth had described.

Whatever could be wrong? Were her parents ill? Had there been an accident? Was someone chasing her? Kathleen took Sharly's trembling hand and led her inside. "Come in and tell us what's happened."

Sharly followed Kathleen inside and sat down at the kitchen table. "They—they surrounded our house with fiery torches . . . and thr-threatened to burn us out." Sharly's voice shook as she talked.

By now the whole family had gathered in the kitchen, eager to know what was going on.

"Who has threatened you? When?" Uncle John asked.

"Right now—awful men dressed in white robes." Fear was etched on her face. "I was out in the barn when they came—twenty or thirty of them. They burned a cross in our front yard." Her voice broke and she sobbed.

"It's the KKK." Uncle John's eyes narrowed. "That's what I was afraid of. Try to remember everything, Sharly—what did they say? What all did you see before you came here?"

"Men in robes, they placed a cross in our front yard. They lit it with their torches. They—they threatened to harm anyone who left the house. They said we had been con-condemned, and they were going to burn our farm to the ground." Once again, tears welled up in Sharly's eyes. She looked at Aunt Elizabeth. "I would have stayed in the barn, but when I saw them heading my direction with torches, I sneaked out the back window and hid in the field. But those men—"

Kathleen had never seen such terror on anyone's face. Grandma Maggie brought a glass of cold water and handed it to Sharly. She drank several gulps. Gaining strength, she went on. "They walked past the barn and directly toward me—as if they had seen me."

"Did they?" Papa asked.

"No, sir, I don't think so—I got up and ran across the field to your place before they got too close. I turned to look behind me just before coming over the hill to your field and all I saw was a wall of fire."

"They've set your wheat on fire!" Alex exclaimed. "I'll go harness the team—maybe we can save some of the crop."

"Do—do you think they will set our house on fire?" Sharly's eyes were full of fear.

"I hope not. We'll go over there first and see to it the KKK leave immediately—if they haven't already. We'll make sure that no one has been harmed," Bruce said.

"The car—it will get us there faster," Papa said, dashing out the door to fetch his keys from Grandpa's house.

"I'm coming too—who knows what fright Mrs. Williams has just been through," Mama said.

"Bruce, you and Alex load up the wagon with supplies in case the fire gets out of control. We'll meet you there," Uncle John said. Kathleen could hear the concern in his voice. "With the fields as dry as they are and as windy as it is tonight . . . who knows how far the fire will spread before it stops."

"Yes, sir." Bruce turned toward the girls. "Lindsay, you, Kathleen, and Sharly go find some empty burlap bags, shovels, anything that we can use to beat out the fire. Robby and Richard, go gather all the buckets and barrels you can find and load them in the wagon.

"Mom, I'm going to the barn, and then out to fight the fire." Bruce stopped to look tenderly into his mother's eyes. "You okay here? Is there anything I can do to help you hold down Stonehaven while we're gone? With the winds the way they are, that fire might come up toward our house—you'll need to dig trenches and drench the ground around the house."

Aunt Elizabeth stood on her tiptoes and quickly kissed Bruce on the cheek.

"I'll be fine, son. Just promise me you'll take care of yourself . . . and take care of Robby; he thinks he can handle a man-sized job."

Within seconds everyone was heading in different directions preparing for action. When Kathleen and Lindsay ran out to the barn in search of empty feed sacks and shovels, they saw the red glow of the flames reflected in the sky. Kathleen's thoughts went back to the KKK ritual that she and Robby had stumbled upon a couple of months before and she shuddered. These men were frightfully wicked! She could not believe they would harm the Williamses.

Poor Sharly! She had never seen anyone look so scared. Kathleen's heart burned at the injustice.

Lindsay had already picked up an armful of empty feed bags. She pointed to the corner of the tack room. "If you plan on fighting the fire in the field, you had better bring a long-handled shovel and some burlap bags . . . there's no telling what sort of fight you'll face."

"I don't care how tough the fight is as long as we win." Kathleen grabbed a shovel. "I can't believe that any human being would do such a terrible thing." Her face grew hot with anger.

"Bruce just asked me, Richard, and Robby to stay back at the farm and start digging a trench around the

farmhouses—just in case the wind carries the fire up this far," Lindsay said, as Kathleen climbed in the back of the wagon.

"A trench?" Kathleen questioned.

"Yes, so we can fill it with water to keep the fire from jumping over," Lindsay yelled as the wagon jolted to a start.

Oh, a moat, how clever. The wagon pulled away into the darkness of the night.

"Be careful!" Lindsay's voice faded as Bruce and Alex drove the team of horses into a full gallop.

Kathleen held onto the sides of the wagon as they raced blindly down the road. Suddenly, the reality of the situation hit Kathleen.

Dear Lord, what am I doing? I'm racing out to fight a field fire, and I don't know the first thing about putting one out—especially one this huge. Please give me Your strength and protection.

Kathleen slowly felt her way in the darkness and climbed through the back of the bouncing wagon. Finally she reached the front buckboard where Bruce and Alex were seated. Kathleen stood up behind the seat. Much to her astonishment, the road in front of them was completely black—there was no moon out. She could not even see the outline of the road. The only thing she could see was the fiery glow in the distance, coming from the direction of the Williamses' field.

Kathleen's Enduring Faith

"Can the horses see where we are going?" Kathleen shouted in great alarm.

"Kathleen! What are you doing back there?" Alex asked in astonishment. "I mean, I thought you stayed back at the house to help dig the trench."

"I wanted to help you stomp out the fire." Kathleen clutched the back of their seat so tightly she was sure her knuckles were white. The thud of the horses' hooves, the loud creaking and jolting of the wagon, and the wind blowing swiftly past her ears made it hard to hear even her own voice. At that precise moment, she was convinced they would never make it to the field because they were racing down the road at breakneck speed in pitch darkness. "It's too dark to see! How do you even know if we are on the road?" She tried to sound as if she were not really scared, but her voice sounded a bit alarmed.

"The horses know where the road is," Bruce yelled over his shoulder. "We'll make it there just fine. The real question is, when we get to the Williamses', will we be able to stop the fire?" His voice sounded strained, as if he, too, was anxious about what lie ahead.

They crested the hill and were able to get a full view of the Williamses' field for the first time. Kathleen gasped. The fire had spread to over a hundred yards across and flames shot up at least five feet

into the air. The hungry flames were headed up the hill toward the McKenzie's field.

"Look at that!" Alex pointed at the glow in the distance, which had suddenly grown larger. "The wind is carrying it toward our place."

"It's moving fast," Bruce shouted.

Kathleen stared at the blazing flames. She imagined herself in its midst, trying in vain to stop the raging inferno. What if she were to suddenly become surrounded in the fire and be unable to fight her way out?

Dear Lord, please give me courage and strength. In Your Word You promise that Your strength is made perfect in our weakness, and I feel very weak right now.

The blazing red flames whipped and lashed, quenching the last bit of moisture left in the dry field. The fire hungrily consumed the wheat in its angry grip before it raced on, looking for its next victim.

Alex turned the horses off the main road and drove them up the Williamses' drive. The team raced toward the farmhouse. Kathleen was grateful to see that neither the house nor barn had been set on fire. Papa, Uncle John, and Mr. Williams rushed out to meet them, carrying shovels, garden hoes, buckets—anything they could find that might help stop the fire.

"Thanks be to God that you have come!" Mr. Williams cried.

Kathleen's Enduring Faith

"Climb on! There's not a moment to lose." Bruce reached his hand down and helped Mr. Williams climb into the back of the wagon.

"Kathleen? What are you doing here?" Papa asked in surprise when he saw her.

"I came to p-put out the fire," Kathleen answered. "I didn't know how big it was. Do you think I can help?"

"Of course you can—just beat the flames down with a shovel or wet burlap. But be careful! Stay close to the far edge of the field near the river or the road." The team of horses galloped straight toward the flames. Papa had to talk loudly in order to be heard over the noisy wagon. "Don't get surrounded by the flames or cut off from the rest of us. If ever you get lost and feel threatened by the fire, just wade out into the river and wait there—or find a shallow spot and cross over."

Bruce pulled the horses to a stop near the flames. As they piled out of the wagon, the heavy smoke fumes surrounded them. Kathleen coughed. She had smelled the smoke before, but now her eyes burned and her throat felt scorched—almost as if it too were on fire.

"Bruce, take the wagon down to the river, fill up the buckets and troughs, and wet all the burlap bags. The rest of us will start beating back the flames with what we have," Uncle John shouted as he grabbed a shovel out of the back.

"Kathleen," said Papa, "go with Bruce and help with the water—and be careful. Never let your guard down; fires are unpredictable." Papa quickly helped Kathleen back into the wagon. As he did, he whispered in her ear, "God bless you, lass. Your papa's so proud of you."

Kathleen's eyes filled with tears. She wanted to blame them on the smoke, but she knew better. Something about his sincere, somber words struck her heart and opened her eyes to the seriousness and danger of this fire.

He thinks we are in grave danger. What if—what if something were to happen . . . those could be the last words I ever hear him speak.

"Thank you, Papa!" Kathleen waved at her papa as he pulled a handkerchief up over his face and headed toward the leaping flames that were devouring the wheat. "I love you." Her words melted into the crackling of the fire and soon the darkness surrounded her as the wagon swept her away from her papa.

Race Against the Flames

*Fear not, for I have redeemed you; I have summoned you by name;
you are mine. . . . When you walk through the fire,
you will not be burned; the flames will not set you ablaze.*

ISAIAH 43:1–2

"Are you frightened, Kathleen?" Bruce asked, taking his eyes off the horses for a moment. His question caught her off guard. To this point everyone's focus had been on fighting the fire, but now Bruce was taking the time to make sure her heart was feeling up for the fight.

"Maybe—a little. The fire looks mighty big compared to us." She clutched the buckboard seat as they hit a rut in the field. Instead of heading around the field on the road, Bruce had decided to cut straight through it to the river. The fire was far enough away as it was.

"Lass, God has us all in the palm of His loving hand, and if He chooses to carry one of the McKenzie Clan to the celestial city tonight, then we will wake up on the streets of gold. I, for one, wouldn't mind being the first," Bruce said with an accent that sounded a lot like Grandpa's. "That's what Grandpa used to tell me when I was a wee lad and I was frightened at the thought of dying. I used to dread the thought of leaving this earth—but not anymore. I'm at peace with my Maker," Bruce said confidently. "Of course, I would miss my courageous cousin, Kathleen."

"I'd miss you too, Bruce." Kathleen smiled. Somehow, Bruce referring to her as being brave gave Kathleen courage.

He pulled the team to a stop at the river. "We better hurry." Bruce's voice was serious again and Kathleen knew he understood the urgency of the situation far more than she did. Knowing this, it especially blessed Kathleen that he had taken time to encourage her.

Kathleen raced down to the river, dipped her bucket in the water, and carried it as fast as she could back to the wagon where she dumped it into a large water trough in the back. By the time the trough was full, Kathleen had blisters on her hands from the heavy buckets. But that didn't stop her. Next she and Bruce wet the burlap bags and filled every bucket. Soon they were making their way back across the field.

Kathleen's Enduring Faith

Bruce drove slowly in an obvious attempt to keep from spilling all the water, but Kathleen could hear it sloshing back and forth with each bump and wondered how much would be left.

Soon they crested a hill that gave them full view of the fire. "It doesn't look like they have made much headway," Kathleen said as she looked at the blazing glow that covered most of the Williamses' wheat field.

"It's because of the wind. It's too strong to hold the fire back," Bruce said. "Hopefully the water will help—what we have left of it."

Thankfully they still had some water left by the time they reached the others. Bruce situated the wagon at the edge of the field, near the road, but as close as possible to where the rest were fighting the fire. That way they could run back and forth to the water source.

At first, Kathleen stayed with the wagon keeping the horses calm. When she felt she could leave them for a moment, she drenched fresh burlap bags in the trough and periodically exchanged them with the dried out ones the men had returned. The wet burlap seemed to help a little—but not enough. Kathleen watched in amazement at the men's tireless fight. No matter how heavily they panted or how drenched they were with sweat and soot, they pressed on.

The horses stomped and snorted and pawed at the ground with fear. Kathleen tried talking softly to

them and gently stroked their necks to calm them. She even tried turning the wagon so their backs were to the fire. But they could still hear the raging fire and yelling men. Kathleen was on the verge of losing control of them, when Alex noticed.

"Kathleen, do you think you can take a turn fighting the fire?" he called out as he approached the wagon. "The horses are used to me — I think I can settle them."

"Yes . . . yes, I can fight the fire," Kathleen answered confidently. But her hands shook with nervousness as she drenched a burlap bag and realized that this time it was for herself. Suddenly, a verse from the book of Isaiah that she'd memorized several years before came to her mind: *Fear not, for I have redeemed you; I have summoned you by name; you are mine. . . . When you walk through the fire, you will not be burned; the flames will not set you ablaze.*

"Thank You, Lord, for bringing that to mind. Thank You for promising to be with me as I walk through this fire," Kathleen whispered. She then ran with renewed courage toward the flames. Choosing a spot near her papa, Kathleen beat the base of the fire as she had watched the others do. The flames in front of her sputtered, appeared to be going out, then sprang back to life, snapping and popping — stronger than before. Kathleen beat a spot of fire, throwing all her strength into each blow. She felt triumphant as she watched as the blaze sputtered and died. She looked up only to gaze into a whole new patch of burning wheat.

Without faltering, Kathleen moved on to the next spot and then the next. She ran to soak her burlap bag in the water trough and noticed she was dripping in sweat and covered with soot. After several trips, the coarse burlap bags had rubbed her blistered hands raw. Kathleen hardly noticed—there was no time to stop and take care of them.

"We're about out of water, Kathleen," Alex called when she returned to the wagon for the fifth time. "You and Mr. Williams come with me to the river." He motioned to Mr. Williams, who was running up behind Kathleen. "You can fight the fire on that side of the field with shovels while I fill the trough. The wind must have switched directions. The fire seems to be heading toward the river now."

Once in the wagon, Kathleen had a better view of the fire and could see the new direction the flames were moving. It was true; the wind was pushing the fire more toward the river instead of up the hill. Kathleen felt a glimmer of hope. The fire had already moved too far in the direction of Stonehaven—if it went much farther it would cross into their wheat field and head straight for the barn, then the houses.

"All we have to do is keep it heading toward the river," Kathleen said. "Then it will have no choice but to die out."

"That would be a great mercy—let's hope the wind doesn't change direction again," Alex said, clucking at the horses to move forward even though they wanted to turn and run in the opposite direction.

Just before reaching the river, Mr. Williams pointed. "Kathleen, why don't you get off here with me and fight the edge of the fire—we'll try to keep it heading in the direction of the river." Alex stopped the horses long enough for Kathleen and Mr. Williams to jump off and then he quickly drove the horses to the river.

Kathleen and Mr. Williams began beating the edge of the wall of fire, trying to keep it burning toward the river.

Before long, they were in the middle of the field halfway between the river and the road. Realizing she was standing on the same side of the field where the fire was furiously heading just minutes before made Kathleen nervous. She kept thinking of Papa's caution about not letting the fire get between her and the river or the road so she would not get cut off from an escape route.

Surely, we are safe now that the fire has switched directions. Kathleen stopped to wipe the sweat from her forehead that was dripping into her already burning eyes. She looked around. If the fire were to turn suddenly, Kathleen knew the only hope for escape would be to outrun the fire by heading up the hill toward

Kathleen's Enduring Faith

Stonehaven—which was at least a quarter of a mile away. She was too deep into the field to reach the river or the road. Kathleen looked over her shoulder to make sure that Mr. Williams was still close by.

Kathleen kept beating back the fire with her shovel and tried not to get discouraged at the lack of headway they were making. Looking down at her stinging hands, she saw that her blisters were now bleeding. The sweat dripping down her arms made them sting even worse. She could not tell if her eyes wouldn't stop watering from the pain she was trying to ignore or from the smoke that seemed to envelop her.

The smoke all at once grew thicker. She glanced around, trying to figure out why. On both sides, Kathleen was surrounded by flames. The glaring flames looked like arms reaching out, groping to devour anything in their path. The wind had changed directions. The fire was heading straight toward Kathleen.

Her legs felt like rubber. She knew she must run, but she couldn't move. She was surrounded by flames on all but one side. Mr. Williams was nowhere in sight. Kathleen's only hope was to drop her shovel and run for her life.

Dear Lord, please let me make it to Stonehaven. I must make it safely. I must warn the others . . .

8

Tragedy

*Blessed is the man who perseveres under trial, because when he has
stood the test, he will receive the crown of life that God has
promised to those who love him.*

JAMES 1:12

Kathleen turned and raced toward Stonehaven. The flames were ten feet away on either side of her and were closing in quickly. The heat was like an oven. Her lungs ached for cool, fresh air. In a few quick strides that felt like an eternity, Kathleen raced out in front of the wall of fire, but the waist-high wheat slowed her down. Kathleen ran as fast as she could, but still she felt and heard the roaring flames. No matter how hard she ran, the wind blew harder, keeping the wild fire on her heels. Finally, when Kathleen wasn't sure if she could run any faster, the flames suddenly slowed their pace, enabling Kathleen to make considerable headway.

When she reached the top of the hill and crossed over into their field, Kathleen glanced over her shoulder. She'd gained over a hundred yards, but the fire was still headed in her direction. Kathleen looked in front of her at the flickering lantern lights coming from Stonehaven. The barn was a little over two hundred yards ahead and the houses not far beyond that.

"Dear God, help us. We have to think of a way to keep our houses from burning to the ground," she cried aloud as she pressed on. Kathleen arrived at the barn completely out of breath and black with soot. Her dress was torn in several places and her stockings ripped.

Mama and Aunt Elizabeth were digging a small moat around the houses and Lindsay, Richard, and Robby were dashing to and from the pump house with buckets of water to fill the trench. Grandpa and Grandma Maggie were pumping water and filling the buckets as fast as they were emptied. Everyone was so busy they did not notice Kathleen appear from out of the darkness of the field.

"The fire! It's coming!" Kathleen shouted as she broke into the lantern-lit barnyard. Her aunt and mama looked up from their digging.

"Kathleen! Are you alright? Where's your papa?" Mama dropped her shovel and gasped in astonishment.

Kathleen was relieved to see that her mama had returned from the Williamses'—that meant that Sharly's family was safe.

"He's fighting the fire—it's just over the hill and coming this way. We have to get the animals out of the barn." Kathleen heaved, trying to catch her breath.

Lindsay and Sharly came from across the barn-yard where they were hauling water to fill the ditches that now almost surrounded the houses.

"Do we have time to dig a ditch around the barn?" Lindsay asked as she poured a bucket of water into the channel.

"No—there's only time to save the animals and supplies," Kathleen said. She turned to race toward the barn and smacked into Richard, knocking him and the full bucket he carried to the ground. He was completely drenched in water.

"Richard—I didn't see you." Kathleen reached her hand out to help him up.

"What happened to you?" Richard stood and stared at the hand Kathleen used to help him up. "What's that black stuff all over you and your hands— they're covered in blood!"

"You look like you've been fighting a war," Robby said as he ran by carrying an empty bucket back to the pump house.

"I have been and the battle's not over. We have to do something quickly. The fire is coming this way. We have to get the animals out of the barn."

By this time Grandpa and Grandma had seen Kathleen from where they were manning the pump

house and had rushed over. "Kathleen is right; we need to save the animals," Grandpa said. "Robby, you and Richard take the cows to the shallow part of the river. Lead them to the other side and tie them up. Then come back for the pigs. Lindsay, you and the girls lead the horses down and then come back for the sheep. Just turn the chickens loose — they'll be fine! We'll finish filling the trenches with water. There is so little grass around the houses that I pray they will be spared. But the wheat field backs right up to the barn."

Kathleen turned toward the barn, but Grandma Maggie stopped her. "How are you holding up, dearie?" She put her hand on Kathleen's shoulder. "Your hands are bleeding so and your dress is torn and black with soot. Why don't you let me see to those cuts?"

"Not now, Grandma, later." Kathleen gave her hand a reassuring squeeze. She hoped Grandma did not notice her grimace.

Soon the barnyard became a flurry of activity. Kathleen first went to Nellie's stall and grabbed her and the filly by the halter and led them down the road and safely across the river. Then the girls had their hands full trying to keep the herd of cows from stampeding down the road. It was evident they could sense danger in the air.

From the high bank of the river, Kathleen could tell that the fire had reached their field. The girls ran as fast as they could back to the house, but by the time they

returned to the barnyard, the flames were lapping against the back of the barn and climbing up the morning glory vines that grew up the sides. Papa and the men were fighting the fire around the back side of the barn. Thankfully, the trenches managed to keep the fire away from the houses, and the fire was blocked off by roads on all the other sides. If they could just stop the fire at the back of the barn, maybe they could get it under control.

This sudden ray of hope gave Kathleen enough courage and strength to storm right back into the fight. She helped clear the rest of the animals out of the barn. Now all they had time to do was open the doors to the pens and chicken coop and hope the rest of the animals were smart enough to fend for themselves. Then she helped Bruce move as much gear and supplies out as possible.

"We're losing the barn," Bruce yelled through the smoke. "Clear out."

Kathleen and Bruce carried out the last armload of saddle blankets, bridles, and harnesses. Once they were out of harm's way, they stopped to watch as the great beams holding up the structure began to pop and crack as they were consumed by flames.

"Thank God, we are all out safely—and the animals too." Kathleen breathed deeply.

Kathleen heard yelping from inside the barn somewhere. "Spunky is still in there," she cried, starting to run back in.

Kathleen's Enduring Faith

"No—no, it's too late. You'll never make it." Bruce grabbed her arm. Just then burning timbers near the back corner of the barn gave way. Kathleen thought she heard Robby's voice. She was too mesmerized by the flaming barn to stop and look around the barnyard. When the sparks settled from the falling timber, Kathleen saw where the voice was coming from. Fear clutched her heart. Robby was in the barn making his way through the debris with the puppy wrapped tightly in his arms.

"Run, Robby! Run for your life!" Bruce cried.

Robby was too frightened. He stood frozen and disoriented by the falling timbers.

"Stay here!" Bruce yelled to Kathleen. He dashed through the flaming door.

Kathleen watched in horror as the timber just above Robby started to give way.

Bruce saw it too. He thrust Robby's head out of harm's way by diving in between the crashing timber and Robby. The large timber landed on Bruce and Robby, pinning them both to the floor of the barn.

Kathleen screamed and ran into the barn to free them before the whole building collapsed. The heat was intense and it was difficult to see. Robby's legs were pinned by a much smaller beam. He still clasped his puppy tightly in his arms. She was immediately able to free Robby, but his pant legs were dark red with blood and he couldn't walk.

She turned and tried to pull the large beam off of Bruce. It barely moved. The weight was too great.

"No, Kathleen. The barn's coming down," Bruce managed to murmur despite the pain from the weight bearing down on his body. "Gr-grab Robby and g-get out before . . ."

"I can't leave you here — Help, somebody, help!" A sob welled up in Kathleen's throat. Above her she heard cracking, and she knew each second was precious.

"Leave — save Robby! He — he can't make it out by himself," Bruce gasped.

Kathleen turned to see Robby lying on the barn floor, clinging to his puppy with one arm, and trying to pull his body along the floor with the other. Bruce was right. She could not save them both. Kathleen ran to Robby, and putting her hands beneath his underarms, she half carried, half dragged him from the barn.

Robby was struggling to look back and was crying. "Bruce! Bruce! No . . . no . . ."

Kathleen heard a loud crash behind them, and she knew what was happening. Uncle John, Papa, and Grandpa raced toward them, leaving the fire line that they'd been fighting at the trench.

Uncle John took Robby from her and scooped him up into his strong arms. "Robby, are you okay? What has happened?"

"Bruce, Bruce!" Robby sobbed and reached back toward the barn.

"What is it? Where is Bruce?" Uncle John looked from Robby to the collapsing barn.

"He's inside," Kathleen cried with tears streaming down her face. The barn had collapsed on two sides now and what was left of the structure was tilting far to the side, about to completely give way.

"No—" Uncle John yelled. Without taking his eyes off the blazing barn, he laid Robby down on the ground and attempted to run into the flames to find Bruce, but Papa stopped him.

"It's too late," Papa said firmly, his voice choked with emotion. He secured Uncle John by the shoulders and looked him straight in the eye. "It's too late. You can't go in there."

The main beam cracked for the last time. A huge gush of hot wind and billowing sparks swept toward them as the barn collapsed. Kathleen looked away— unable to watch. She turned and fell to her knees next to Robby, who lay helplessly on the ground. His tears streaked a path through his soot-stained face. He had let go of Spunky and was just staring blankly toward the barn.

"Br-Bruce is, Bruce is gone . . . and it's my fault," Robby sobbed.

Kathleen took him into her arms. "Hush, Robby, you—must not say that. Bruce wouldn't want you to.

Tragedy

He—he was ready to go home to glory—he told me so." Hot tears flowed down Kathleen's face as she recalled their conversation about Heaven earlier that night. Kathleen closed her eyes.

Bruce knew it was his time—he was trying to tell me so. Lord, thank You for giving him that peace. But Lord, this is so hard, so very hard—please give us strength.

Even though the whole McKenzie family was numbed by Bruce's tragic death, they knew there was nothing they could do about it. They had to press on; they had to keep the fire away from their homes. After the accident, Robby was carefully placed in the backseat of the Chevrolet and Papa drove him and his parents to the doctor in town. Kathleen went back to fighting the flames. As she worked, she heard various family members crying sorrowfully as they struggled against the flames. Sometime before dawn, they were successful. The last of the flames were extinguished. Three of the wheat fields, two of the corn fields, the houses, and all the out buildings were saved. But the barn was completely gone. It had burned to the ground. All that was left was a heap of smoldering ashes riddled with glowing embers.

As the early lines of morning formed on the horizon, painting the sky in light hues of pink and yellow, Kathleen dragged herself into the house and up the stairs to bed. She felt numb and empty as she lay down on her bed. She had never felt so spent—worn out emotionally and physically. Lindsay was already fast asleep next to her, her puffy eyes evidence that she had been crying.

Kathleen heard Spunky howling out on the porch as if he too understood the loss. Her thoughts turned to little Robby and how badly injured his legs looked. She wondered if they would ever completely heal.

Please, Lord, encourage his heart. Don't let him feel guilty for Bruce's death.

That was all Kathleen could manage to pray. She was trying to be strong in her faith, but there was so much she didn't understand. Kathleen's heart ached with an unexplainable feeling of loss and sorrow. She tried to reject the fact that Bruce was really gone, but deep down she felt it. She kept replaying in her mind the events leading up to the tragedy. Surely there was something she could have done to save Bruce. Hot tears trickled down her face. Dwelling on it was not helping. It was too late. Nothing could be done now. Kathleen muffled her sobs in her pillow until she was totally spent. Sleep finally came.

When Kathleen woke up the sun was high in the sky. The events of the night before still seemed like a blur. Kathleen rushed downstairs to see if Papa, Uncle John, and Aunt Elizabeth had returned with Robby from the doctor. Kathleen was anxious to

know how he was doing. Grandma Maggie was at the stove slowly stirring some porridge she was making for lunch. She looked weak and tired. Kathleen wondered if she had slept at all since last night.

"How is Robby?" Kathleen asked.

"I wish I knew, lass. We haven't heard a word." Grandma Maggie looked up from the pot she was stirring. "But take heart, lassie. I imagine they'll be home any minute now." Grandma smiled, but Kathleen could tell it was strained. Kathleen knew she was worried. If only they had a way to communicate. More than ever, Kathleen wished there was a telephone at the farm.

Robby's Return

Let the morning bring me word of your unfailing love,
for I have put my trust in you. Show me the way I should go,
for to you I lift up my soul.

PSALM 143:8

The afternoon sun beat down on Kathleen, Lindsay, and Richard as they watered the parched garden. In the two weeks that had passed since the fire it still had not rained. Kathleen brushed her hair out of her eyes with her free hand and searched the horizon for any sign of the farm wagon. Beyond the charred field there was a dust cloud, but she could not tell if it was kicked up by wagon wheels or merely loose dirt riding the wind. Kathleen looked back down at the bucket in her hand and slowly drizzled water onto the wilted tomato bush.

Kathleen's thoughts turned to Bruce. It had seemed like the entire population of Archbold and the

94

surrounding farms showed up for his memorial service. Kathleen had no idea that there were so many people in the community who had been touched by Bruce's life. Kathleen was struggling to understand why God would allow something like this to happen. She remembered Pastor Scott's words: "Though our hearts are saddened at the loss of Bruce's life, those of us who are Christians can rejoice in the knowledge that it is only temporary and that we will see him again in Heaven. In our finite comprehension of God's perfect will, we may struggle to understand why He would take such a wonderful young man home to be with Him so early in life. But God looks at death in a completely different light. In Psalm 116:15 it says, 'Precious in the sight of the LORD is the death of his saints.' God loves His children and has prepared a wonderful place for Bruce with Him. Though we will miss him dearly, our hearts can rest and even be glad to know that he is in Heaven—a place that is more glorious and wonderful than we could ever comprehend with our earthly understanding."

Kathleen stopped watering for a moment and looked up toward Heaven.

Dear Lord, I do thank You that Bruce is with You and that he is happy, but please help me to trust Your timing in taking him home.

Kathleen continued to water. Her thoughts drifted back over the events of the past two weeks. Pastor

Kathleen's Enduring Faith

Scott, his wife, and the whole church community had shown immense support to Kathleen's family and to the Williamses in their time of disaster and loss. Since Bruce's death, a day had not gone by without one family or another from the congregation dropping off a hot cooked meal, baked bread, or fresh produce from their gardens. The drought was hard on everyone in the community, but that did not deter the kindness and generosity of their church members.

Kathleen later found out that the night of the accident, Papa had gone immediately to Sheriff Ratcliff and reported that the Ku Klux Klan had burned a cross and started the fire in the Williamses' field, which ultimately led to Bruce's death. The sheriff said he had kept his eyes open all summer for any suspicious behavior. He already had several suspects that he thought might have been involved and promised to investigate the case directly. Within a week, the sheriff had made several arrests and felt that he had sufficient evidence to convict the men. Kathleen was thankful to know that the sheriff was working hard to bring the people responsible to justice. She hoped and prayed that all the guilty men would be caught before they harmed anyone else.

Kathleen sighed. "I can't wait for your parents to get back from town with Robby. It's just not the same around here without him."

"Not the same at all." Richard kicked a clump of dried dirt. Spunky chased after it. He'd been following

Robby's Return

Richard around ever since Robby had left, never leaving his side. He obviously missed Robby just as much as everyone else.

"I'm glad Dr. Rogers is finally letting him come home," Lindsay said. Her eyes looked sad despite the smile she bravely displayed. Dr. Rogers had been concerned that Robby's burned, crushed legs would develop gangrene. He insisted that Robby should stay in town at his house to keep a close watch on him. Thankfully, his legs were healing nicely and there was no longer a risk of having to amputate, but Dr. Rogers did not give much hope that Robby would ever walk again.

Kathleen put her bucket down and rolled up her blouse's sleeves. "I don't care if I get sunburned. It's too hot to work with long sleeves. I wonder if it will ever rain." She peered up at the sky looking for clouds, but all that met her gaze was the blistering sun with its relentless burning rays.

"I've never seen it so dry," said Lindsay. "Even the fruit on the apple tree outside my window is shrunk and shriveled. Normally this time of year we have enough fruit to make quarts of applesauce, apple butter, and tons of apple pies loaded so thick with juicy fruit that they overflow. But this year . . . if we save all the apples down in the cellar, hopefully we'll have enough to make a couple of pies for Thanksgiving. Bruce loves—" Her voice broke. "I mean loved—my apple pies. He would always say Thanksgiving dinner would not be complete without one." Lindsay stopped weeding, leaned against the hoe, and stared at the horizon.

Kathleen could tell she was trying not to cry. Bruce's death had been the hardest loss Kathleen had ever experienced, not only for her, but the whole family. His name would often come up in conversations as if he were still alive.

Kathleen looked over at the empty patch of land where the barn once stood. It looked barren. Her eyes filled with tears. Every time she saw the empty spot, it would remind her of the horrible fire and how much she missed Bruce. Kathleen couldn't wait until a new barn was built. Perhaps then she wouldn't think of Bruce's death so much. Uncle John had already cleared the area and marked the site with stakes in preparation for building a new one. Nobody said it, but Kathleen knew they did not have the money to buy lumber for a barn. The Williamses had offered to let them use their barn to store the supplies that had been rescued and to house the chickens and smaller livestock, but Kathleen knew they must have a barn by harvest and that was only a month away—that is, if there was a harvest. And what about winter? The livestock would freeze to death if they didn't have shelter.

All these thoughts stormed through Kathleen's head. The weight of the burden that hung over her

multiplied in the heat of the day. She trudged back to the water pump to refill her bucket. She pumped the water and watched as a thin stream flowed slowly into the bucket.

"Home, sweet home!" a familiar voice called out above the noise of bustling wagon wheels.

Kathleen looked up. A broad smile spread across her face. It was Uncle John. He had returned from town with Robby. She sat the bucket down and ran to greet them.

Kathleen reached the wagon at the same time Uncle John parked the team next to the back door. She couldn't see Robby. Had something happened? Had he gotten worse?

Richard and Lindsay rushed around the side of the house. Spunky barked happily as he ran beside them.

"Where is Robby? Didn't he get to come home?" Kathleen searched Uncle John's face eagerly.

"He's back here with me." Aunt Elizabeth stood from the bed of the wagon. Kathleen, followed by Lindsay, Richard, and Spunky, rushed around the wagon to unlatch the back gate. Kathleen prepared herself for what she was about to see. She must be strong for Robby's sake. She had to keep up her courage and trust everything would turn out just fine. If she didn't, Robby would sense that something was wrong. Kathleen drew a quick breath when she first saw Robby. His legs were wrapped up in bandages

99

and propped up by boards. His face was pale and it was obvious he'd lost a lot of weight. His frail features made him look younger, and yet the pained expression and grief that he wore made Robby look aged. There was a moment of silence as they took it all in. Finally, Kathleen burst out excitedly, "Welcome home, Robby! We have all missed you so much!"

"It's nice to see you too, Kathleen," Robby whispered feebly.

"Hi, Robby. I took good care of Spunky while you were gone. He's gained at least three pounds." Richard scooped up Spunky and handed the puppy to Robby. Spunky barked and wagged his tail in excitement. "He's saying it's been pretty dull around here without you."

"Thanks, Richard, I missed both of you, too." Robby hugged Spunky tightly and let him lick his face. "You have grown, haven't you, boy!" Robby's eyes were full of pain.

Lindsay, who seemed to be in shock at the sight of her brother's weakened state, finally found her voice. With forced gaiety, she said, "We've decided to cook a special meal in honor of your homecoming—all you have to do is tell us what you want and we'll have it ready by suppertime."

Robby's eyes showed a glimmer of life. "Can I really have *anything* I want?" he asked, looking at his mother.

Lindsay glanced at her mother for approval and then back to Robby. "Anything that we have is yours for dinner," Lindsay said.

Kathleen was surprised by Lindsay's promise. What if he asked for something like strawberry ice cream? But she could tell by Robby's reaction it had been exactly what he needed.

Robby looked at Grandma Maggie as she approached the wagon, wiping her hands on her apron. "I've missed Grandma Maggie's chicken 'n' dumplings and sugar cookies, and I've been aching for an apple pie." His voice sounded a bit stronger.

"Well, laddie, I've already made you a batch of sugar cookies." Grandma Maggie planted a kiss on his forehead. "They are baking right now."

Kathleen was glad they could at least offer him the cookies, but the rest of his request? She looked at Aunt Elizabeth with concern. She knew it would be crazy to butcher one of their chickens at a time like this, and all the apples on their tree had withered long ago.

Aunt Elizabeth placed her finger over her lips to motion for them to be quiet, and she moved toward Robby with a steady smile. "That sounds like a perfect homecoming feast. Let's get you inside so we can get started."

Uncle John carried Robby inside and situated him comfortably on a cot Kathleen had helped prepare for

him in the living room so he could be in the middle of family life.

"Your mom thought you might prefer to be down here during the day rather than confined in your room," Kathleen said as she pulled back the covers. Uncle John gently laid him down.

"This'll be great. Dr. and Mrs. Rogers were nice enough, but the only time I got to visit with anyone was when Victoria came by."

"Victoria?" Kathleen plumped a pillow and put it under his head. "Who, pray tell, is she?"

"No one. Just a six-year-old little girl."

"She is the Rogers' granddaughter," Aunt Elizabeth said. "Victoria and Robby became friends."

"I guess she was nice enough. She'd bring me candy and tell me stories. Seemed kind of odd that she wanted to play with me."

"I think she's an only child. She was probably lonely like you." Aunt Elizabeth covered Robby's legs with a quilt.

Kathleen brushed Robby's curly red hair out of his eyes. "There's no reason for you to be lonely now. From here you can see what's going on in the front yard and in the kitchen. And, should you have any needs, all you have to do is ring." Kathleen picked up a small bell she had found in Grandma Maggie's attic. "We are here to attend to your wishes, Sir Robert. You are now the gallant prince of Stonehaven, injured in battle, and we are here to serve you." Kathleen knew he liked stories of the gallant princes of old. He always drank up every word when she read stories of knights in shining armor to him.

Robby smiled, but then he grimaced in pain. He shifted his weight trying to get comfortable. Everyone except Kathleen had gone back to their work. A shadow came over his whole countenance and his eyes looked sorrowful.

"Kathleen, I'm not the gallant prince. You and Bruce were the brave and daring ones . . ." His voice drifted off and he gazed out the window. "You were there — in the barn — it's my fault Bruce died, isn't it?" Robby buried his head in his pillow and sobbed.

"Hush! You shouldn't say such things — Bruce wouldn't want you to think that way." Kathleen gently placed her finger over Robby's pale lips. She paused a moment, asking God for wisdom. "You were very brave to go into the barn, but you would never have gone in the barn to save Spunky if you knew how dangerous it was — would you?"

"No." Robby shook his head, wiping his tears on his sleeve.

"Bruce loved you so much that he would have never been able to live a happy life knowing that he could have saved you but wasn't brave enough. Besides that, it was Bruce's time to go home. God could have taken you or me just as easily — we barely escaped—but it wasn't our time. God still has a plan for us on earth, but Bruce, he was, as he said to me, 'ready to meet his Maker.' He told me so that night before it all happened." Kathleen's throat tightened. She remembered some of his last words to her. She would never forget the love in his eyes and the peace that was so evident despite the situation.

"Robby, the Bible says, 'Greater love has no man than to lay down his life for a friend.' Bruce loved you, Robby, and he would be sad to know you are blaming yourself for his death. If—if Bruce were here right now, he would want you to be brave and strong in your heart and to be healed up soon." Kathleen could not say another word about Bruce—it was too painful. Thankfully, Robby seemed to soak in every word Kathleen had spoken.

His freckled face and green eyes lit up. "Do you think—do you think Bruce would want me to try to walk again? Dr. Rogers says I probably never will, but I can't help but think that Bruce would tell me that I could do it if I try hard enough."

"Yes, Robby, I think that's exactly what Bruce would say. You just think on that while I finish my chores and help your mom and Lindsay make you the best homecoming dinner ever."

Kathleen rushed out the front door and headed back toward the vegetable garden. She needed to gather her composure before she talked to anyone. It

was all so hard. She was trying to be strong, but seeing Robby so pale and crippled, coupled with him talking about Bruce, brought the whole accident back. Tears streamed down her face as she finished watering the garden.

"Why? Why, did all this have to happen? Why has God allowed all these trials?" she cried out loud. "I'm trying to be strong, but when will relief come? Will it ever rain again? When will Papa get a job? Where will we get the money to build a new barn?"

Deep in her heart Kathleen knew she needed to trust God with her fears, but she was so weary — weary of being strong and confident.

"I will be strong. I have to be," Kathleen said resolutely. She completed watering the thirsty garden and headed for the kitchen. Mama was baking bread and Aunt Elizabeth was busy making dough for chicken and dumplings.

"Where are we getting the chicken?" Kathleen asked in surprise.

"I've sent Lindsay and Richard over to the Williamses' barn to butcher one of our hens. I know we can't spare one, but Robby is so weak and frail — I'll do anything to keep from losing him too," Aunt Elizabeth said, her voice full of emotion. "I only wish we had some way of getting apples for a pie. They have them at the general store in town, but they are far too expensive."

Kathleen's Enduring Faith

"Do we have eggs to trade for apples?" Kathleen asked.

"No. Mr. Williams said the hens have not been laying much since the fire. I suppose they're still getting used to living in a new coop. Hens are like that—they get frazzled easily and then won't lay until they are settled again."

"We'll give the desire for apples to the Lord—He is our Provider and we can trust in Him," Mama said.

Kathleen knew her mama was right. She should commit it to prayer, but for some reason her heart revolted at the thought of praying for apples. Kathleen felt bad about her lack of faith, but she felt weary of trusting God for the big things, let alone something as small as providing apples for dinner.

Richard burst through the door. "You won't believe it. We have the biggest, fattest chicken in the whole county! Mr. Williams asked if they could join the welcome home party tonight, and when Lindsay said they could, he insisted on providing their prized rooster that they were fattening up to show at the county fair. He said it was the least they could do. And boy oh boy, I've never seen such a fat rooster in all my born days," Richard said.

Mama shot a look of disapproval at him from across the room—he knew better than to use slang like that, but when he pulled the plucked chicken out

from behind his back, even Mama forgot about correcting his language.

"Glory be! That *is* the biggest chicken I've ever seen." Aunt Elizabeth clasped her hands together. "God bless the Williamses. If they only knew how much this means to us . . ." Her words faded as she examined the juicy rooster. "This will make a fine welcome home meal."

A Welcome Home Feast

*May the God of hope fill you with all joy and peace as you
trust in him, so that you may overflow with hope by the power of
the Holy Spirit.*

ROMANS 15:13

Mrs. Williams and Sharly arrived early, bringing a basket of vegetables from their garden and another one full of assorted baked goods from the kitchen.

"We thought we would come over and help with dinner preparations." Mrs. Williams beamed. "Sharly's got a basketful of goodies to tempt Robby's appetite. There's no telling how many different tasty treats are in there—she's been baking all afternoon. Now, before I roll up my sleeves and get to work, I'd like to say hello to Robby."

Aunt Elizabeth led the way to Robby's cot, while Kathleen helped Sharly unload the basket filled with chocolate muffins, cinnamon rolls, gingersnaps, a Southern pecan pie, and an assortment of baked sweet breads.

"How did you ever come up with this food?" Kathleen asked. She suspected the Williamses would probably eat slimly for the next two weeks as a result of their generosity.

"God provided some of this through the kindness of your church members, and the least we can do is share it with you all," said Sharly. "Goodness, Kathleen, if it weren't for the McKenzie family, we'd probably be packed up and headed down South where we came from—and Dad says there isn't much of a future for us there. I'm just glad we can return the favor." Sharly placed the pecan pie in the pie safe.

Kathleen smiled. She remembered back when she first met Sharly—there wasn't much left of the timid, frightened girl. Now that Kathleen had won her trust, Sharly was as spunky and confident as any girl.

Dinner turned into a feast. There was plenty of food to go around and more love shared than most of the world could imagine. Robby's pale face brightened into a smile throughout the whole evening and there was laughter once again at Stonehaven. Robby was finishing his plate of seconds when a knock came at the front door.

"I wonder who that could be?" Grandma Maggie asked as she ladled a few more creamy dumplings on Robby's plate.

"Maybe it's Dr. Rogers, but I didn't think that he was calling to check up on Robby until morning." Aunt Elizabeth rose to answer the door. Everyone turned to see who it was as Aunt Elizabeth opened it.

It was Pastor Scott's son, William. He held a large basket in his hands.

"Good evening, William. You've come just in time. Robby has come home today and we're celebrating," she said, swinging the door wide open.

"Thank you, I would be delighted. Your celebration makes my offering perfect." He handed Aunt Elizabeth the basket. As he spoke, his eyes eagerly scanned the room until they fastened on Lindsay's rosy face.

Kathleen looked at Lindsay in time to catch her surprised expression turn into a deep blush.

"Can I take your basket to the kitchen?" Aunt Elizabeth asked, trying to regain his attention. Kathleen could tell she knew the cause of his great distraction and was trying her best to hide her smile.

"Oh! Yes—the kitchen would be appropriate— that is, unless you all would like to eat it for dessert. My mom baked several apple pies and insisted on sending a couple of them out your way."

Kathleen's mouth dropped open. She could not believe what she had just heard. Mrs. Scott must have spent a fortune at the general store buying enough

apples to make apple pies. She didn't think they had apples on their trees either.

"How perfect!" Joy spread across Aunt Elizabeth's face and she looked over at Robby's cot. He wore a smile as broad as his face. "Isn't that just like God, Robby? He has sent you an apple pie even in the middle of this drought. Wherever did your mother find the apples?" Aunt Elizabeth looked back toward William with tears glistening in her eyes.

"My Aunt Augusta sent them. She lives in New York City and says you can buy bushels of them on the streets for pennies," William said. "But I've been so distracted by your invitation to dinner and talking about apple pie that I've forgotten to tell you the real reason for my visit." William produced an envelope from his pants pocket.

"The men have come together and decided to hold a barn raising next week before harvest time. Here's money that our church members donated to help with the supplies and lumber costs." William handed the gift to Uncle John.

He fingered it. His chin quivered and his eyes filled with moisture, revealing his overwhelming gratitude. "Tell your father . . . and the men at church . . . the McKenzie Clan is most grateful." His voice was tight with emotion and his words few, but no one in the room doubted his sincerity.

Kathleen's Enduring Faith

Kathleen looked at Sharly, who was sitting across the table from her. From her grin she could see that the Williamses already knew about the barn raising.

Grandpa McKenzie stood up and motioned for William to take a seat. "Please, join us for supper. We're almost finished eating, but we have plenty."

Kathleen's heart went from pure joy to sudden feelings of shame. She had been so discouraged and weary of trusting God to supply their needs, yet He had once again faithfully provided for not only their largest needs but also their smallest desire.

After the last of the dinner dishes were cleared and the guests had left, Kathleen headed over to Grandpa McKenzie's house.

She knocked softly on her parents' bedroom door. "Papa, Mama, are you still awake?"

"Yes, dear, come in," her mother answered.

"I need to talk to you," Kathleen said.

"What's on your heart, lass?" Papa kissed his daughter on her freckled forehead as Kathleen sat down on their bed and gathered her thoughts.

"I'm not sure where to begin—so much has happened in the last few weeks. But somewhere in the midst of all the trials we've been through, I began to grow weary of trusting God to provide. Not that I didn't think He could, but I was beginning to think that He just didn't care about us anymore. I knew deep in my heart that these thoughts were straight

from the devil and so wrong, but the doubts crept up so slowly I cannot tell when they came. But ever since Bruce was killed in the fire, I've had a harder time praying and asking God for anything. I've tried to be strong—but it's been in my own strength and the burden has been far too great to bear." Kathleen bit her lip to keep from crying. "Mama, today when you said that we needed to trust God to provide apples for Robby's pie, I even resented the thought of prayer. But tonight when God not only provided apple pies for dinner, but also the means to build a new barn, I felt so ashamed of my recent attitude and lack of faith. Now I feel so undeserving and discouraged that I was so weak." Kathleen hung her head and soft sobs shook her body.

"Kathleen, you have no need to be discouraged," said Mama. "Realizing your weakness and having a contrite heart—though it is never easy—is precious in God's eyes. You should be sorrowful for your sin, but rejoicing even more that God has proven to be faithful, despite your lack of faith." Mama hugged Kathleen tightly until her sobs died down.

"Kathleen," said Papa, "your mother and I could not be more pleased with you. God has brought us through numerous trials this past year, but in the Bible it says that the Lord disciplines those He loves. This discipline is not always a direct result of disobedience—I like to think of it as God's boot camp. We're His soldiers and

Kathleen's Enduring Faith

He's perfecting us so that we will shine in this dark world. Just as gold that has been refined many times in the fire always shines brighter, God allows fiery trials in our life to perfect our faith. It may be hard, but we should never resent this, Kathleen. Remember, He is the author and finisher of our faith—we may never understand, but we can trust Him."

"Yes, Papa, I remember the lesson I learned last summer. We are to run the race of life with perseverance." Kathleen paused and thought for a moment. "I have been running hard, but—but that's it!" she exclaimed. "I've been running the race, but relying on my own strength instead of the Lord's strength. I have not been keeping my eyes on Jesus. How could I forget something so simple?"

"I wouldn't be too hard on yourself, Kathleen," Mama said. "Sometimes the simplest sounding principles we learn in the Scriptures are the hardest ones to live up to on a daily basis."

"That's why we have to keep our eyes on Jesus and spend time in the Word drawing from His strength." Papa looked at her curiously. "While we are on the subject of trusting God, I have a special prayer request. I've just received a letter from the life insurance company that I visited with last winter, after our car was stolen."

"What did it say?" Kathleen sat straight up in anticipation.

"They are hiring again and liked what they saw in my résumé—"

"Does that mean you have a job?" Kathleen interrupted.

"Well, not yet, but they would like for me to come in for an interview. It's scheduled for next Monday."

"When will you know if they want to hire you?" Kathleen's eyes sparkled with renewed hope. She had almost given up the idea of ever returning to Fort Wayne, but now that the hope was rekindled, she ached to be back home. How Kathleen longed to see Lucy, Freddie Schmitt, and all her friends at school. She would miss Stonehaven and her relatives, who had grown so dear, but the thought of returning to her own home—the neighborhood, church, and school where she grew up in—had grown to be a dream too good to be true.

"The earliest I could know whether or not I have been hired is Monday after my interview, but don't count on it. Sometimes big companies like that take weeks before they come to a decision," Papa said, "and there are hundreds of applicants."

Next Monday was almost a week away—Kathleen could hardly bear the thought of waiting any longer. Immediately, Kathleen chided herself. Had she not just a few minutes before been reminded to stop trusting in her own strength? God would give her the grace and patience to wait. She needed only to ask

Him in faith. In the meantime, she should focus her prayers on asking God for rain and relying on the Lord to give her the right words of wisdom to encourage Robby as he adjusted to being crippled.

Kathleen's heart felt lighter than it had since Bruce's death as she made her way back to Uncle John's house. Her heart was so merry now that she was trusting God again that she started singing aloud.

What a Friend we have in Jesus,
all our sins and griefs to bear!
What a privilege to carry
everything to God in prayer!

Oh, what peace we often forfeit,
Oh, what needless pain we bear,
All because we do not carry
everything to God in prayer.

Have we trials and temptations?
Is there trouble anywhere?
We should never be discouraged;
take it to the Lord in prayer.

Can we find a friend so faithful
who will all our sorrows share?
Jesus knows our every weakness;
take it to the Lord in prayer.

When Kathleen reached the bedroom she shared with Lindsay, she saw that her cousin had already fallen fast asleep. Too bad—she had hoped to ask her how her evening with William had gone. She wanted to know how Lindsay had hidden her true feelings this time. She loved Lindsay and knew that even though her cousin denied it, deep down, Lindsay really did like it when Kathleen teased her.

Kathleen quietly pulled her flour sack nightgown over her head, blew out the candle, and slipped into bed. The morning would come early—they always did on the farm. Kathleen was determined to wake up earlier than usual. She planned to spend extra time reading her Bible and praying.

"I want to start my day with my eyes focused in the right direction," Kathleen whispered in the darkness. She rolled over and slipped into a deep, peaceful sleep.

A Refreshed Spirit

I will refresh the weary and satisfy the faint.
JEREMIAH 31:25

Throughout the next week, Kathleen was up before the sun peeked its head over the eastern horizon so she could spend time reading the Word, praying for rain, and pleading with God to heal Robby's legs so he could walk. As the sun slowly rose, she eagerly searched the horizon for any sign of rain. But with each new day, the fields looked drier than the day before. By the time Papa was packed and ready to head for Fort Wayne Friday evening, the crops looked as though they would soon shrivel up and die if something miraculous did not happen soon.

"Don't despair, lass," Papa said, affectionately running his finger down her nose. "God makes all things beautiful in His time. He ordains when the rains will come, and He knows when I'll get a steady job."

"I won't worry." Kathleen smiled. "But I have to admit, I am awfully glad that you have over two days to get to Fort Wayne this time — that way even if your car is stolen, you'll still be able to make it in time."

"I would hope so." Papa laughed. "Remember, God knows best — He had a plan to have us here at the farm this summer. Kathleen, think on it a while — if you had not been here during the fire, Bruce wouldn't have been the only one killed — you saved Robby's life."

Kathleen caught her breath. She had not thought about it in that light. She had just done what she knew was right. All at once she was overwhelmed with gratitude to the Lord for allowing them to be living at the farm for so long. Tears came to her eyes. "You are right — God knew what He was doing."

"That's the spirit." Papa gave Kathleen one last hug and turned to say good-bye to Richard and Mama.

"Papa?" Kathleen asked.

Papa looked back toward her.

"I've also been praying that Robby could walk again. I know the doctor said it was impossible without an expensive series of surgeries from a big city specialist and even then, doubtful. But I want to believe differently. He's so young and full of life . . . I can't bear to picture him an invalid the rest of his life."

A shadow crossed over Papa's face. It *was* a hard thought to accept. But as quickly as the shadow came, it left again. "It's not wrong to pray and hope for the best. All things are possible with God."

Later that evening, Kathleen joined Robby on his living room cot to see if he wanted her to read to him.

Robby's face brightened at her suggestion. "May we read that book you and Lindsay were talking about—the one with the brave man who risked his life during the French Revolution to save innocent people from Madame Guilly—guil-la-tine or whatever that French word is."

"You're talking about *The Scarlet Pimpernel*, the story of the man who was able to rescue people right from under the very noses of the tower prison guards, leaving no sign of his whereabouts except a note sealed with the crest of a humble wayside flower," Kathleen said with exaggerated grandeur. She loved the story of this wealthy man who left his comfortable home in England and risked his life at the hands of the crazed French populace in order that he might save a few innocent people from being beheaded by the guillotine. She loved how he performed these noble acts, yet no one knew his true identity.

Kathleen read to Robby until late in the evening and his eyes were no longer able to stay open. Kathleen rose and was about to blow out the candle

and tiptoe out of the room when Robby turned his head toward her and opened his eyes.

"Kathleen, do you think I will ever walk again? I know what Dr. Rogers says, but what do you think? Do you think that if I pray every day, God will heal me?" Robby's blue eyes looked at her in earnest.

Kathleen slowly sat back down on his cot.

Dear Lord, give me wisdom. I know You can heal him if that is Your will, but how can I explain that to Robby?

Kathleen took a deep breath and took his hand in hers. "Robby, I think it is right for you to hope and pray that God will heal your legs. I believe that God can heal them—no matter what the doctor says."

"I knew you would say that. I think that's what Bruce would tell me too if he were here. He'd tell me to keep my chin up and keep trying," Robby said with somber determination.

"Yes, Robby, you must keep your chin up—up so that your eyes are fixed on the Lord Jesus. He's the ultimate Physician and can heal you in a moment if He wills it, but sometimes God allows difficulties in our lives for reasons that we don't always understand. You must keep in mind that He makes all things beautiful in His timing. God even has a purpose for you being in bed right now."

"He does? He has a purpose for me right now while I'm lying here with my legs propped up? How could God make something good come from being stuck in this cot?" Robby asked sincerely.

"I know He has a plan for you and a good purpose. In Jeremiah 29:11 there is a promise that I read just yesterday morning. I liked it so much that I read it over and over until I memorized it. The verse says, '"For I know the plans I have for you," declares the LORD, "plans to prosper you and not to harm you, plans to give you hope and a future."'"

"That's nice. Will you help me memorize it too? Then I will be able to say it every time I get sad about being bedridden." Robby seemed comforted by hearing the verse. Kathleen was touched by his childlike faith and trust.

"Of course. We'll say it together again in the morning." Kathleen brushed his red hair back from his forehead and smiled. "Good night, Robby. May you be blessed with sweet dreams of Jesus."

Kathleen lay in bed for some time before she was able to fall asleep. Even though she was sleepy, Kathleen felt such a burden to pray for Robby and for rain that her mind would not rest.

Dear Lord, please heal Robby's legs. Let him walk again. His faith is as it should be—childlike and trusting—he believes You can heal him. Please let there be some way for him to see one of those specialists that Dr. Rogers spoke of. I know we don't have the money to send him to a big city hospital, but dear Lord, I know that You do. You've already provided an apple pie, the

means to build a barn, and possibly a new job opportunity for my papa. Surely You could heal Robby, or maybe allow it to rain so that our crops won't die—then maybe we will have enough money to send Robby to see a specialist. Kathleen sighed. *Dear Heavenly Father, I know You have a plan and I don't need to figure things out for You, but please, Lord, however You want to do it—please heal Robby.*

Somewhere in the darkness of the night Kathleen became aware of a light tapping on the rooftop. The noise sounded familiar, but she could not quite place it. Kathleen rolled over and pulled the covers around her neck. Whatever it was, the soft patter was a welcome, soothing sound. After some time, it grew a little louder and tapped more often. Kathleen was not sure if she had fallen asleep yet or if she were just dreaming, but the noise reminded her of rain and quieted her heart.

Thank You, Lord, for settling my heart. I think I will be able to sleep soundly now.

Kathleen took a deep breath, rolled over, and fell deep into sleep. Early the next morning, she was awakened by Lindsay shaking her excitedly.

"Kathleen, Kathleen, it's—"

"Have I slept in?" Kathleen asked drowsily. She sat up and rubbed her eyes. "Lindsay, you won't believe what I dreamed about last night. It was wonderful. I dreamed it was raining all night long—a light, steady rain that was perfect for the crops."

123

Kathleen's Enduring Faith

"You weren't dreaming. It's raining!" Lindsay pulled on Kathleen's arm. "Get up and see!"

Kathleen dropped her hands from her eyes and looked at Lindsay with a puzzled expression. "I wasn't dreaming?"

"Look out the window!" Lindsay pointed toward the windowpane that was glazed over with moisture.

Kathleen's mouth dropped open, and she became aware of the light tapping on the roof that she had heard in the middle of the night. A burst of joy welled up in her heart and a broad smile broke across her face. She jumped up and threw her arms around Lindsay.

"It really *is* raining. The Lord has answered our prayers!" Kathleen exclaimed. Both girls laughed with glee and danced around the room.

Kathleen abruptly stopped. "Lindsay, I have a marvelously splendid idea. Let's hurry and dress and go play in the rain!"

"I've never heard of such a thing," Lindsay said, shaking her head.

"I'm sure you haven't. You also said you've never seen a drought like the one we've just been through. Therefore, I say it is time to celebrate! Let's do it — just this once." Kathleen pulled her nightgown over her head and quickly changed into an older dress.

Before long the girls and Richard were running wildly through the yard and around the house slipping and sliding in the mud until every inch of them was

covered. They washed off by standing under the steady flow of water rushing out of the porch's rain gutter. Then they returned to run and slip and slide in the mud all over again. Kathleen and Lindsay played until they were soaked to the bone, and they laughed until their sides ached.

"Rain, glorious rain," Kathleen said as she and Lindsay changed into dry clothes Aunt Elizabeth had provided for them. "Back in the city, I hardly thought twice when it rained. Now it seems more glorious than a Christmas present!"

The soft, nourishing rain continued Saturday, Sunday, and on into Monday. It was light enough that it didn't damage the crops and constant enough to soak the earth with its gentle touch and nurture the parched harvest until each stalk of wheat stood strong and straight in the field. By Tuesday afternoon, the day Papa was supposed to return, the rain had slowed to a drizzle, but the dirt road leading up to Stonehaven was far too muddy for a four-wheeled vehicle.

All morning Kathleen had been anxiously watching out the living room window for his return. "How will Papa get home?" Kathleen stopped writing a letter she was composing to Lucy and looked up at Mama.

"The rain and mud might slow him down but not stop him." Mama smiled. She was darning a pair of

Richard's socks. "You know Papa; he would never stay away from us a day longer than he absolutely had to."

Kathleen looked down the empty road. She could hardly wait for Papa to return. She longed to know how his job interview had gone. Kathleen was about to get back to washing the dishes when she saw a black object appear and then disappear in the distance. It appeared again, but she could not make out its true identity in the foggy mist. It was too small to be a car. It looked more the size of Lindsay's filly, yet it didn't move like an animal.

Could it be Papa? Would he have parked his car out by the highway? Kathleen dropped the dishrag, then dashed from the kitchen across the living room, out the front door, and up the driveway.

"It is Papa!" Kathleen exclaimed as she ran through the mud and rain to greet him. "Papa! God has answered our prayers. It's been raining for days now, and the crops have been spared. We will have a harvest!" Kathleen called as she neared him.

Papa had his coat wrapped closely around him, his hands pressed deep into the pockets, and his hat pulled down over his face to keep from getting too wet. When he heard Kathleen's voice, he pushed his hat back and opened his arms out wide to embrace her. "Yes! I see it's been raining. I had to park my car a good mile away or I'd have sunk in the mud."

Kathleen jumped into his arms and he swung her around in a circle like he had when she was a little girl. "How is my Kathleen? I have such wonderful news—I couldn't wait to tell you. Not even the rain and mud could stop me." He placed her back on her feet.

"Did they hire you?" Kathleen asked. Tears of joy sprang up in her eyes and a lump formed in her throat. She already knew the answer. Kathleen could tell by the twinkle in her papa's eyes. He had not looked so happy and carefree in months.

"First, before I tell you that, I must let you know that I stopped by Sir Willaby Wallace's place in Fairview, and he wanted me to let you know about his newfound faith in Christ—he said that God used our visit that day to get his attention, and he's been a changed man ever since!"

"Oh, Papa! That's wonderful!" Kathleen clasped her hands together in joy.

"And to answer your question about my job interview, yes, Kathleen, they hired me. I start next month. We'll move back to Fort Wayne directly after helping the family with the harvest—and after the county fair, of course. We have to stay long enough to see if Elias's pig, Blue Boy, lives up to his name." Papa put his arm around Kathleen and they started toward home. "That isn't all my news, little lass, and it's not nearly the best part either."

Kathleen's Enduring Faith

Kathleen stared at Papa. His face looked relaxed and carefree, like it had before the stock market had crashed and he'd lost his job. Everything was turning out so wonderfully well. What other good news could he possibly have? "Whatever could be better than that?"

"I visited a long time with Dr. Schmitt about Robby, and he sent me to a specialist at Indiana University. The long and short of it is that the staff was very sympathetic to Robby's case, and they'd like to take him on—free of charge! There are no guarantees that the surgeries will work, but they were very hopeful."

Kathleen froze in her tracks; her heart felt like it would explode with joy. "Papa, the Lord has answered our prayers above and beyond anything we could have imagined!" Grabbing Papa's hand, she ran ahead, pulling him along. "Come on, Papa! Let's run. I can't wait to tell Robby and the others!"